Snowbirds and Suspects

Sapphire Beach Cozy Mystery Series
(Book 5)

Angela K. Ryan

John Paul Publishing

TEWKSBURY, MASSACHUSETTS

Angela K. Ryan
John Paul Publishing
Post Office Box 283
Tewksbury, MA 01876

Publisher's Note: This is a work of fiction. Names, characters, places, and incidents are a product of the author's imagination. Locales and public names are sometimes used for atmospheric purposes. Any resemblance to actual people, living or dead, or to businesses, companies, events, institutions, or locales is completely coincidental.

Cover Design © 2019 MariahSinclair.com
Book Layout © 2017 BookDesignTemplates.com

Snowbirds and Suspects/ Angela K. Ryan. -- 1st ed.
ISBN: 978-1-7340876-4-2

A Note of Thanks from the Author

I would like to warmly thank all those who generously shared their time and knowledge in the research of this book, especially:

Jacki Strategos, Premier Sotheby's
International Realty, Marco Island

Carol Buccieri
Bella Stella Beads, Haverhill, Massachusetts

Marco Island Fire Rescue
Marco Island, Florida

Any errors are my own.

Chapter 1

A LOUD KNOCK on the glass behind her nearly caused Connie Petretta to drop the necklace she was arranging in the display window of her jewelry shop, *Just Jewelry.* Connie literally laughed out loud when she turned to find Ruby Boyd, her friend and owner of the souvenir shop next door, enthusiastically waving and pointing to the front door of Connie's shop with one of her crutches.

Connie nodded to indicate that she would meet her at the front door. She cautiously scooted out of the tight space where she was working and greeted Ruby, careful not to knock over any of the displays.

Grace, who was Connie's friend, neighbor, and part-time employee, had been ringing up a customer and joined the two women.

"What's all the excitement for?" Grace asked. Grace and Ruby had become fast friends in the ten months since Connie opened *Just Jewelry*. The two regularly took lunch breaks together to eat at the beach, which was just a couple of short blocks away.

Ruby hobbled over to the long oak table, where Connie often created jewelry or taught jewelry-making classes, and Connie and Grace followed. Ruby leaned her crutches against the table and took a seat. "I am so excited," Ruby announced. "I have a niece!"

Connie and Grace exchanged a confused glance. As far as Connie knew, all of Ruby's siblings were well beyond childbearing age.

But Ruby continued undeterred. "I'm going to meet her tonight for dinner." She looked wide-eyed at Connie and Grace apparently awaiting their reaction.

Grace put her arm around Ruby's shoulders. "Slow down, my friend. You're not making any sense. I know you have a niece and two nephews, but how is that exciting news?"

Ruby laughed and took a deep breath. "Let me start over. For my birthday my brother, Glen, bought me one of those DNA kits - you know, so I could trace our family lineage. I sent a DNA sample in, and it turns out we have a niece that we didn't know about. Her name is Amy. She is thirty years old and lives in Fort Myers. Apparently, she got some type of notification after I did the DNA test, so she reached out to me online a couple of weeks ago. We got to talking over email, which led to some extensive phone conversations. It turns out that Amy is the daughter of my brother, Kevin."

Grace appeared to be searching her memory. "You mean your brother who passed away?"

Ruby bobbed her head up and down. "That's right. Kevin had a fatal heart attack four years ago at the age of fifty-two. But isn't it wonderful that he had a daughter we never knew about? She seems like an amazing young woman from what I could tell over the phone. She's an elementary school teacher, and she is engaged to a man named Peter who sounds terrific."

"That's amazing," Connie said, warmly embracing Ruby. "I'm so happy for you."

"Did Kevin know that he had a daughter?" Grace asked.

"No. According to Amy, her mother never told him about her. I suppose I should be angry about that, but I'm just so excited to learn about Amy that there's just no room in my heart for anger."

"If Amy is from Fort Myers, how did your brother know her mother? Isn't your family from Wisconsin?"

"Judging from Amy's age, they had to have met when my brother was in law school. During that time, he spent summers working as a waiter in Sapphire Beach and living at our family's former vacation home, where I now live. My family has been coming to Sapphire Beach since I was a little girl. When my parents died ten years ago, they left the family's vacation cottage to me, my brothers Kevin and Glen, and my sister Tammy. I decided to move here permanently for a fresh start, so I bought out my siblings and opened the souvenir shop. All of my remaining siblings ended up buying their own second homes in Sapphire Beach, and they all spend their winters here."

"Wasn't Kevin married?" Grace asked.

"Yes. I haven't told his widow, Sally, about Amy yet. I figured I'd meet Amy in person first and get to know her before introducing her to the rest of the family. I'm not sure how Sally will feel about Amy. She and Kevin married later in life, and they don't have any children. Amy was born long before they even met."

"That's wild," Connie said. "With technology today, stories like this are becoming increasingly more common. With more and more people signing up, ancestry databases are growing. More people are finding long lost family members or family they didn't even know existed."

Grace smiled. "Well, if you're happy, then I'm happy. Just remember, there are a lot of crazy people in the world, you know. Promise me you'll meet this woman in a public place. If anything goes wrong, it's not like you could run very far with that sprained ankle."

Ruby waved Grace off. "I'm telling you, there is nothing to worry about. Amy is a sweetheart, and I can't wait to meet her in person. But if it makes you feel any better, we're meeting at Gallagher's Tropical Shack for dinner tonight, so we won't be alone."

Connie was pleased to learn that, since Gallagher's was right across the street.

"In that case, I wish you a wonderful evening," Grace said. "I can't wait to hear all about it."

"I'll say a prayer that it turns out the way you hope," Connie said.

"Well, I'd better get going. I have a few things to do in my shop before meeting Amy tonight, and everything takes longer with these crutches."

"That'll teach you not to climb on ladders when you're alone," Grace said.

"It could have happened to anybody," Ruby said. Then she left *Just Jewelry* wearing the same broad smile she came in with.

"It's wonderful to see Ruby so happy," Grace said. "I'm just crossing my fingers that she isn't disappointed."

Connie agreed. "I'd hate to see Ruby get hurt. She does so much to make others happy. When she learned I was selling Fair Trade jewelry, she immediately inquired about selling some products from my artisans in her own shop. She said that God blessed her in her life, so she always does what she can to bless others."

"Ruby has a heart of gold. And I get the feeling that heart has been refined in fire. She doesn't talk about her past a lot, so I can't say for sure, but it's just a feeling I get," Grace said. "I hope she finds some happiness connecting with this young woman."

"So do I, but I'm happy they're meeting in a public place," Connie said.

Grace nodded her agreement. "I'm sure there's nothing to worry about, but better safe than sorry."

For the rest of the afternoon Connie and Grace barely had had a free moment. It was the third week in January, and the snowbirds were returning to Sapphire Beach in full force. This meant that a steady stream of customers flowed in and out of the downtown shops for much of the day. Grace was working a double shift to cover for Abby, Connie's other employee and a student at nearby Florida Sands University, so that Abby could attend a concert. Grace's tireless energy never ceased to amaze Connie. Not only did she work part-time for Connie, but she was also training for her next mini-triathlon, which was just a couple of months away. Connie hoped she had that much energy during *her* retirement years.

7

There was a lull in customers around dinnertime, so Connie took advantage to take Ginger, her Cavalier King Charles Spaniel, for a walk. When she returned, Detective Zachary Hughes, whom Connie was dating, was seated on the red sofa in the seating area of her shop.

"I just got off work and was in the neighborhood picking up dinner, so I thought I'd come by to say hello."

Connie unhooked Ginger's leash, and the dog trotted over to greet Zach.

"You two visit. I've got this," Grace said gesturing towards a customer who just walked in.

Connie gave Grace an appreciative smile and joined Zach in the seating area.

He stood to greet her and kissed her on the cheek. "I came downtown to grab a quick dinner, because I'm meeting Elyse tonight to look at some more houses." Elyse, one of Connie's closest friends in Sapphire Beach, was also a realtor and the wife of Detective Josh Miller. "I thought I'd stop in and say hello since I was in the neighborhood."

Connie felt a warm smile spread across her face. "I'm glad you did. It's always nice to see you."

"Actually, I came for another reason as well," Zach confessed. "I know it's still three weeks away, but I was hoping you might be able to break away from the store for dinner on Valentine's Day."

Fortunately, Abby worked on Friday nights, so Connie was hopeful that she would be able to take the time off. "I should be able to, but let me just double check with Abby before I commit."

"Nonsense," Grace chimed in. "If Abby would like to take Valentine's Day off, I am happy to switch a shift with her and come in early. You two make plans."

Grace's voice startled Connie, who hadn't noticed that she was just a few yards away showing a woman around the Fair Trade section of the store.

"I vote for the date," the customer said, winking at Connie and Zach. "It's a holiday for couples, and you two seem to enjoy each other's company."

"You know what they say," Zach said. "The customer is always right."

Connie laughed. "Okay I guess it's settled then."

Zach smiled broadly. "Perfect. I'll make reservations somewhere special."

Zach's phone pinged, and he pulled it from his pocket. "I'd better go. It's Elyse reminding me that we're meeting in her office in five minutes."

The downtown streets began to empty, and before Connie knew it, it was time to close shop.

Just as Connie and Grace were about to flip the 'open' sign to 'closed,' a joyful Ruby came through the door with a young woman who had brown, wavy hair. Connie assumed she was Amy. There was a tangible affection between the two women that indicated they had enjoyed getting acquainted over dinner.

"I just *had* to introduce the two of you to my niece, Amy," Ruby said, grinning from ear to ear.

When Amy smiled, her dark eyes had the same sparkle as Ruby's.

"It's wonderful to meet you," Connie said, shaking Amy's hand.

"It's nice to meet you, too."

Amy looked around *Just Jewelry*. "It's beautiful in here," she said. Her gaze settled on the Fair Trade section. "I love that you support artisans in developing countries. Ruby told me about your store over dinner."

10

"Amy spent two years in the Peace Corps after college, so I was telling her about your work," Ruby said.

"I spent two years volunteering in Kenya with a faith-based organization," Connie said. "That's where I first learned to make jewelry. What country were you in?"

"I worked with children Guatemala. It changed the trajectory of my life, leading me to get a degree in early childhood education. It was the best experience of my life."

"I know exactly what you mean," Connie said. "We'll have to get together and swap stories."

"Definitely," Ruby said, placing a hand on Amy's shoulder and squeezing. "Now that I've found Amy, I don't plan on letting her out of my life. There will be plenty of occasions for that."

Amy's joyful gaze met Ruby's. "The feeling is mutual. I'll definitely be visiting Sapphire Beach on a more regular basis."

Ruby looked at Amy and shook her head. "I still can't get over how much you look like my brother."

Amy smiled and patted her pocketbook. "I have to agree. Thank you for the pictures of my father."

After Ruby and Amy left, the women closed the shop and walked together to the parking lot at the end of the street.

"I guess we were concerned for no reason," Grace said with a chuckle. "Amy seems like a lovely young woman."

"I agree. I'm looking forward to getting to know her."

Chapter 2

THE NEXT MORNING as Connie and Grace were enjoying a steaming cup of coffee before opening the store, Ruby stopped in.

Grace stood to get Ruby a cup of coffee from out back, but Ruby motioned that she didn't want any. "I've already had two cups. I just came by to see what you thought of Amy."

Grace moved Ruby's crutches off to the side, while Ginger sniffed them curiously.

"She seemed lovely," Grace said.

"She's more than that," Ruby said. "I know I said it last night, but she reminds me so much of my brother. It's like being with Kevin again. I was hesitant to submit my DNA to that company, but I'm so happy I did. Things have a funny way of working out."

"I'm sure your brother is smiling down, happy that the two of you found each other," Grace said.

"I know you're right. I could literally feel him with us last night. Connie, I think you and Amy will get along wonderfully. Amy spoke so passionately about her time in the Peace Corps that I just had to introduce the two of you."

Connie nodded and smiled. "I'm looking forward to getting to know her. It's always nice to meet a kindred spirit."

Ruby's phone pinged, indicating that she had received a text message. She pulled her phone from her purse and smiled as she read the text.

"Let me guess," Grace said. "It's from Amy."

"How did you know?" Ruby asked.

"The smile. It's nice to see you so happy."

"After I got home last night, I called my brother's widow, Sally, and we had a long conversation. I was planning to wait a little while before telling her about Amy, but Amy is anxious to meet the rest of the family. So, out of courtesy, since she is my brother's widow, I thought Sally should be the first to meet her."

"How did she take the news of her deceased husband having a child with another woman?" Connie asked.

"Surprisingly well. At first, she was skeptical of Amy's intentions, but once I described Amy and told her how much she reminds me of Kevin, she wanted to meet her as soon as possible. I texted Amy earlier this morning and asked if I could give Sally her phone number, and she enthusiastically agreed." Ruby held up her phone. "That text was from Amy, telling me that the two are meeting at Sally's house for coffee later this afternoon. I couldn't be happier. If their meeting goes well – and I'm sure it will – I can have Amy over to the house soon to meet the rest of the family."

"That's fantastic," Connie said. "Are your siblings in town yet for the winter?"

"My brother, sister, and brother-in-law are snowbirds. They come after New Year's and return to Wisconsin after Easter, so they are already in town. And Sally lives in Sapphire beach full-time. After Kevin passed away, she sold their primary residence back home and moved permanently into their vacation home in Sapphire Beach." Ruby ran a hand through her thin blond hair and let out a deep sigh. "I just hope it goes well when we all get together."

"I don't understand," Grace said. "I thought you said they would love Amy?"

"Oh, it's not Amy. It's my siblings and Sally that I'm concerned about. None of us have remained close to Sally since Kevin died, because, truth be told, she was responsible for his death."

"What do you mean?" Grace asked.

Ruby massaged her bad ankle, then leaned back in her chair. "Kevin was a lawyer, and he worked his fingers to the bone to afford the lifestyle that Sally wanted. When he met Sally, Kevin was working as a federal prosecutor, but he was burnt out. He wanted slow down. When they got married, Sally insisted he switch to a more lucrative job, where he worked just as hard but made a lot more money. He never thought the stress was worth the money, and his dream was to retire early and spend his time volunteering. They certainly had enough money for him to do that, but Sally insisted they buy a large home with a hefty thirty-year mortgage, so he felt trapped." A tear fell down Ruby's cheek. "Tammy and I both think Kevin worked himself to death, but Tammy is the one who can't let it go. It comes up almost every time we're together. I've been trying to forgive Sally, and I thought I had, but I can't help but think that if she hadn't treated my brother like a work horse, he might be alive to meet Amy."

Connie's heart went out to Ruby. That was a tough one to forgive. "At least you took a step in the right direction by telling her about Amy."

Grace nodded encouragingly. "That shows progress."

"I guess you're right," Ruby said between sniffles.

Connie slid her a box of tissues. "You mentioned your brother dreamed of spending his retirement volunteering. Maybe that's where Amy gets her passion for service," Connie said.

Ruby smiled. "I hadn't thought of that, but you could be right."

Connie was pleased to see a smile return to Ruby's face.

"Look at me carrying on like this. I'd better get back to my shop. I just wanted see what the two of you thought of Amy."

"Let us know how Amy's meeting with Sally goes this afternoon," Grace said as she handed Ruby her crutches.

"You bet."

It was another busy day, with a few proactive men stopping by *Just Jewelry* in search of the perfect Valentine's Day gift for their significant other. Connie loved asking just the right questions to help them find that perfect gift.

As usual, Grace left at 1:00 and Abby arrived a few hours later at 4:00. Abby was anxiously waiting to hear from Florida Sands University about whether she was accepted to their doctoral program in American Literature. Connie hoped she would be, even if her reasons weren't entirely altruistic. Abby was a top-notch employee, and Connie wanted her around for several more years. But so far Abby hadn't received any word on her application.

With the steady influx of customers, the day once again flew by. January afternoons were a far cry from the scorching summer months when everyone stayed indoors. Gone were the afternoons when Connie could people-watch through her front window while sipping iced tea or spend a few hours replenishing her jewelry supply. But it was a welcome change. If every year was like this one, she would easily be able to make a good living from her jewelry shop and even hire an additional part-time employee so she could spend more time enjoying southwest Florida's sunny weather.

In between helping customers, Connie loved hearing stories about Abby's undergraduate adventures. In some ways, Connie felt like her college years were just yesterday. But then, in other ways, they seemed like a lifetime ago. Since college, she spent two years in Kenya, worked nearly twelve years for *Feeding the Hungry*, then, more recently, she moved into the Gulf-front condo that her beloved Aunt Concetta left her and opened *Just Jewelry*. And judging from sales the past few months, she would be able to make a good living at it. Indeed, a lot had happened in the nearly fifteen years since she graduated college.

Around dinnertime, business gradually slowed down and the downtown crowd thinned out.

"I can take it from here if you'd like to meet up with your friends earlier than you'd planned," Connie said. Abby had mentioned her plans to watch a movie at a friend's house after work. The shop didn't close until 9:00, but there weren't likely to be many more customers.

"Thanks. I think I'll take you up on that," Abby said.

When Abby left, Connie swept the floors and straightened up, then relaxed on the couch with Ginger on her lap, waiting for 9:00 to arrive.

Just as Connie was about to leave, Grace and a distraught Ruby, hobbling along on her crutches, came into the store. Tears were streaming down Ruby's cheeks, and her hands were trembling.

Connie got her a bottle of water from out back, and Grace led her to the oak table.

"What's going on?" Connie asked, opening the bottle and placing it, along with a box of tissue, in front of Ruby.

Ruby looked at Grace. "You tell her. I'm too upset."

Connie's eyes met Grace's concerned gaze.

"Ruby received a panicked phone call from Amy late this afternoon. When Amy arrived at Sally's house for their coffee meeting, nobody answered the door. Amy said that something didn't feel right. Since the door was open, she went inside and found Sally lying motionless on the ground. She went over to try to wake Sally up, but there was a pool of blood by her head, so she called 911."

"Oh, my goodness," Connie said. "Is Sally okay?"

But judging from Ruby's sobs, Connie feared the worse. Ginger must have sensed Ruby's pain, because she hopped up onto her lap and nuzzled her nose on Ruby's chest. Ruby stroked Ginger's silky fur, as if summoning the strength to say what she needed to say.

"Sally was dead when the police arrived. I just can't imagine who would do this. Amy called me right after she called the police, and I went straight over to try to console her. It's a good thing I sprained my left ankle and can still drive. Amy was too upset to drive, so I dropped her off at the police station to give her statement." Ruby took a sip of water. "If that weren't bad enough, I think the police suspect Amy of killing Sally." She looked at Connie with pleading eyes. "Connie, I know that you have experience with murder investigations. You are the first person I thought of. Promise me you'll do everything you can to clear Amy's name."

Connie had assisted with murder investigations before, but she didn't want to make any promises she couldn't keep, especially since Ruby was in such a fragile state. "I'm not sure what I can do. Detectives Joshua Miller and Zachary Hughes are very thorough. I'm sure they'll get to the bottom of this as soon as possible."

"I promised Amy I'd pick her up at the police station so she could get her car at Sally's, but I wanted to come here first to see if you will help us. I know that the police are capable, but there are only two of them, and for whatever reason, they suspect Amy. You both met her," Ruby said. "Do you really think Amy is capable of murder?"

"I wouldn't think so," Connie said. "She spoke passionately about her time in the Peace Corps, and she struck me as sincere." It didn't mean it was impossible, but Connie's instincts were usually pretty good. "Besides, what motive would she have for killing Sally?"

"Exactly," Ruby said.

"I'll tell you what. Let's pick up Amy together and try to learn more." Connie hoped a conversation with Amy would restore Ruby's faith in the police.

Ruby lept up and hugged Connie, practically knocking Ginger onto the floor.

"Thank you. Let's go," Ruby said, scratching the dog's head to apologize for startling her.

Ginger graciously accepted with a wave of her tail.

Chapter 3

BY THE TIME Connie, Grace, and Ruby entered the waiting room of the Sapphire Beach Police Station, Amy had finished giving her statement and was anxious to leave.

"I haven't eaten dinner yet," Connie said when they got into the car. "How about if we talk things over at Gallagher's?"

Everyone agreed.

They made a quick stop at Sally's so Amy could retrieve her car, then headed over to the restaurant, where they requested to be seated at a relatively quiet table in the corner. Connie ordered a turkey club, while the other three women ordered a couple of appetizers to share, since Grace had already eaten dinner, and Ruby and Amy were too nervous to eat much.

"You poor thing," Ruby said to Amy after they placed their order. "I can't imagine what you've been through tonight."

"Thank you for picking me up," Amy said. "After all the questions from the police, it's nice to see some friendly faces."

"Don't you worry about a thing," Ruby said. "We're going to figure out exactly what happened to Sally, aren't we, Connie?"

How could Connie refuse?

"Why don't we start at the beginning," Connie suggested. "Amy, what happened when you arrived at Sally's?"

Amy shrugged and shook her head. "I told Ruby everything earlier. I had plans to meet with Sally for coffee at her house. When I arrived, I rang the doorbell, but there was no answer. My first thought was that she forgot about our plans or lost track of time, so I sent her a text saying I was at the front door. She didn't respond, so I sat on the doorstep and waited a few minutes, hoping she'd reply to my text. After a while, I thought to look through one of the little windows on the garage door to see if her car was there, and it was. Once I realized she was likely in the house, I began to get nervous. I thought maybe she had fallen and needed help, so I tried to open the front door." Amy's voice began to crack. "I was surprised that it was unlocked." Amy covered her face with her hands and wept.

Ruby scooted her chair closer Amy so she could put her arm around the young woman, and Amy leaned her head against Ruby's shoulder.

"I'm sorry to make you go through this again," Connie said. "You must be emotionally exhausted after finding Sally and talking to the police. Maybe we should do this another night."

"It's okay," Amy said. "It helps to talk about it. As I was saying, I entered the house and was about to call out Sally's name when I saw her lying on the ground. I rushed over to see what happened. That's when I noticed a puddle of blood around her head and called 911 immediately. Then I called Ruby."

Ruby chimed in. "I was there within ten minutes. The police had already arrived and taped off the crime scene, so I couldn't go inside. Josh was questioning Amy in the driveway, and when he finished, she was obviously a mess, so I did my best to console her." Ruby looked at Amy and shook her head. "You poor kid. All you wanted was to learn more about your father, and you walked into that."

"The worst part is that the police think I did it. But why would I hurt Sally? I didn't even know she existed until two weeks ago."

"I know," Ruby said, taking Amy's hand.

Connie spotted Gallagher across the restaurant and waved. He came over to say a quick hello but seemed to notice the gravity of the women's conversation, so he slipped away just as their food arrived and gave them their privacy.

"Amy, it's normal that the police would question you, since you found the body," Connie said. "Given the circumstances, it makes sense that you would be a person of interest. That alone doesn't mean they think you're guilty. Was there anything else they said that led you to believe you were a suspect?"

"It wasn't *what* they asked, it was more *how* they posed their questions," Amy said. "When I went to the police station to give a detailed statement, Detective Miller asked how I knew Sally, so I explained the situation. He was trying to make it sound like I was angry with Sally for my father not being in my life. I assured him that I had no ill feelings toward her. I was excited to meet her so I could learn more about my father and perhaps make a new friend. That's all."

"Can you remember anything else from the crime scene?" Connie asked.

Amy closed her eyes for a few seconds, then opened them again. "I don't think so. Once I saw the body, I was so upset that I didn't exactly survey the scene. All I remember, besides the body, is a wrought iron lamp with blood on it next to Sally. It looked like the killer delivered a fatal blow with the base of the lamp." Amy shivered. "When I saw that, I felt nauseous. I needed to get out of that house, so I waited outside for the police and Ruby to arrive."

After the women finished eating, their server cleared the table, and they each ordered a cup of herbal tea. Although the sun had been strong during the day, it wasn't uncommon for the temperature to drop into the fifties after dark this time of year.

"Let's shift our attention away from the crime scene for now and focus on motive," Connie said. "Ruby, did Sally have any enemies that you know of? Can you think of anyone who would have wanted to harm her?"

Ruby was tearing her cocktail napkin into small pieces.

As soon as Connie asked the question, she remembered what Ruby had said the day before about her sister, Tammy, holding a grudge against Sally because she believed Sally was responsible for Kevin's death. The last thing Connie wanted to do was cause Ruby more pain by adding Tammy to the suspect list. But she had to pursue all avenues. After all, Ruby had asked for her help.

"I know what you're thinking," Ruby said. "But if Tammy wanted to kill Sally because of what she did to my brother, why would she wait four years to do it?" Ruby shook her head. "I'm telling you, you're barking up the wrong tree. It's a waste of time to suspect Tammy when the real killer is out there somewhere."

Ruby had a point. If Tammy were going to do something drastic, she likely would have done it four years ago.

Nonetheless, Connie couldn't help but notice the fear in Ruby's eyes, as if, on level, she believed it was possible.

"What will I do if Tammy goes to jail?" Ruby asked. "I already lost my brother, and now my sister-in-law. I had my problems with Sally, but she was still family and I was trying to move past my bitter feelings. I think Tammy was trying to do the same thing."

"Let's not get ahead of ourselves," Grace said.

Connie nodded her head in agreement. "Grace is right. Let's have a chat with Tammy and at least find out when she last saw Sally. Who knows? Maybe she has a solid alibi and all this worrying is for nothing."

"And she might be able to give us some leads on who Sally's enemies were," Grace said.

Amy had been leaning back in her chair sipping her cup of tea and listening attentively to the conversation. "I feel better now that we have a plan. It may not be much, but at least talking to Tammy will give us a place to start. But if you don't mind, I'm going to sit this conversation out. This is not how I envisioned meeting my aunt."

"Of course," Connie said. "That makes perfect sense."

The server dropped off the check, and Connie snatched it off the table. "You've all been through a lot today. It's the least I can do."

"Thank you," Ruby said. "I'll make arrangements for us to stop by Tammy's house tomorrow afternoon."

"Abby will be coming in at 4:00," Connie said. "If you could arrange a visit after that, Grace and I could both come."

"I'll see if she can meet us at 4:30. I'll call tomorrow and let you know."

Chapter 4

AFTER ATTENDING the 7:00 Mass on Sunday morning, Connie swung back by her condo to pick up Ginger and arrived at *Just Jewelry* in plenty of time for a leisurely walk around town before opening the store at 9:00. She brewed a pot of coffee out back, filled her travel mug, and set out to take in the fresh, salty air. According to the weather forecast, the temperature would climb into the high sixties, but there was still a chill in the air, so Connie threw on her favorite navy blue fleece before heading outside.

Since none of the retail shops had opened yet, the streets were quiet enough to hear the waves crashing on the shore a couple of short blocks away. As she gazed down the street, Connie could see the sun dancing off the clear blue water and was reminded that it had been too long since she took her paddleboard out for a spin. She missed the feeling of paddling down the coastline while seagulls flew past her in flight. After a hectic family visit over Christmas and adjusting to the busier January pace in the store, not to mention two murder investigations thrown into the mix, the bright blue sky and gentle surf beckoned her. She promised herself she would make the effort to go before work some morning soon.

Since it was nearing 9:00, Connie and Ginger made their way back to *Just Jewelry*. Grace arrived a couple of hours later, and the returning snowbirds, thrilled to be back under the Florida sun, kept them on their toes all day. Connie didn't even see the text that Ruby had sent her and Grace, confirming their visit with Tammy at 4:30, until Grace called it to her attention.

Abby arrived a few minutes early for her shift, and, as promised, Ruby picked up Grace and Connie in front of *Just Jewelry* at 4:15. On their way to Tammy's, the three women stopped at Publix to pick up a lemon cake.

When they arrived at Tammy's home, they were greeted by a woman who shared Ruby's dark eyes and light hair, although she wore it longer than Ruby.

After Ruby introduced everyone, the women settled on Tammy's lanai while Ruby sliced the lemon cake they had brought, and Tammy poured hot water into their mugs for tea.

"It's such unfortunate news about Sally," Tammy said, after returning the teapot to the kitchen. I'm still in shock. The police were here earlier asking questions. They said they were interviewing everyone in the family."

"Detective Miller stopped by my shop yesterday to talk with me, as well," Ruby said.

Connie was glad to learn that Josh seemed to be taking the lead on this case. That would give Zach more time to focus on house hunting.

"They asked me a bunch of questions about this Amy woman, the one who found Sally's body. I'm so glad you told me about her yesterday," Tammy said. "Can you imagine if I learned from the police that Kevin had a daughter? I never would have believed it."

Ruby's face dropped. "I hope you don't suspect Amy. She is an angel. There's no way she did this."

"Who else could it be?" Tammy said. "You just met the woman. Maybe she harbored a grudge toward Kevin for not being in her life and decided to take it out on Sally."

Ruby narrowed her eyes. "I don't believe that for a second. Don't even say such a thing. She's your niece."

"Well, I for one, do not want to meet her until they find Sally's killer and I know for sure that it's not her," Tammy said. "I know you were looking forward to introducing us, but I'd rather wait."

"I think Amy feels the same way," Ruby said. "But I can assure you, there's nothing to worry about. She is a lovely young woman. You won't believe how much she looks and acts like Kevin."

"Still," Tammy said, "I'd rather play it safe. And I don't want you seeing her either, Ruby. I can't risk losing my sister. We've been through so much already."

Seeing Ruby's disappointment at her sister's reaction to Amy, Connie changed the subject.

"Would you mind telling us what other questions the police asked you?" Connie asked.

"Oh, the usual stuff you see on television mystery shows," Tammy said. "They wanted to know where I was at the time of the murder, if Sally had any enemies, that sort of thing."

"Were you able to provide them with an alibi?" Ruby asked.

"Unfortunately, no. I was right here on my lanai enjoying the beautiful January afternoon when Sally was murdered. My husband Ray was on the golf course, like he is now, so he can't vouch for my whereabouts. I guess that makes me a suspect."

Connie was surprised that Tammy wasn't showing more sorrow over Sally's murder. The family obviously had their issues with her, but still, murder was something most people didn't wish on their worst enemies.

"Lucky for me, I was working in my shop, so plenty of people saw me," Ruby said.

"What about any enemies?" Connie asked Tammy. "Do you know of anyone who would have benefited from her death?"

Tammy glanced at Ruby, who was looking expectantly at Tammy. "Your friend sure is inquisitive."

"You can trust Connie," Ruby said. "She has a gift for solving mysteries. That's why I asked her to come today."

"I really think you should leave it to the police and not go poking in any hornets' nests," Tammy said.

"I promise we'll be careful. We're just asking around a little bit."

Tammy didn't look convinced, but she continued anyway. "Ruby, you know that I didn't spend a lot of time with Sally. You know how I felt about her. If it weren't for her, Kevin might still be with us. I feel badly that this happened to her, but I can't pretend we were close. I really don't know who she spent her time with."

"I had my issues with her, as well," Ruby said. "But she did seem to change after Kevin passed away. She spent a lot of time volunteering. We even attended some of the fundraisers she organized for Community Food Bank."

"Too little too late, if you ask me," Tammy said.

"You mentioned to me a few weeks ago that you were considering reaching out to her. Did you ever call her?" Ruby asked.

Tammy shook her head. "I thought about it, but in the end, I just couldn't bring myself to do it. I just can't move past what happened to Kevin."

Connie observed Tammy closely as she spoke. There was definitely a bitter edge to her tone, but was she bitter enough to commit murder? Tammy obviously wouldn't admit to visiting Sally if she was the killer. Perhaps she went over to make amends with Sally, but Sally said something to set her off. The fact that the killer used one of Sally's lamps as the murder weapon shows that the murder wasn't premeditated.

"When was the last time you saw Sally?" Grace asked.

Tammy pushed the cake around in her dish with her fork. "I would see her around town occasionally, maybe once or twice a month. We would usually exchange small talk for a few minutes before going our separate ways."

"And she never said anything that struck you as unusual?" Connie asked.

Tammy leaned forward, resting her elbows on the table. "I did run into her at Publix last summer. She mentioned to me that she was dating someone. The way she told me was strange. It was almost as if she wanted permission."

"Kevin passed away four years ago, so it makes sense she would be ready to meet someone else," Ruby said. "And it's understandable that she would have mixed feelings about dating again."

"Do you know anything about the man she was seeing?" Connie asked.

"Not very much. All I know is that his name was Tim and they were dating over the summer. It's possible they weren't even together anymore when Sally died."

Connie let out a sigh. They hadn't learned as much as she'd hoped from their conversation with Tammy.

Connie and Ruby needed to return to work, so Tammy walked the women to the door.

"Are you going to the funeral service?" Ruby asked as they were leaving.

"Yes," Tammy said. "The wake is on Tuesday from 3-7. Ray and I are going and so is Glen. Sally didn't have any living family members, so I think we should stand in the receiving line."

"Of course," Ruby said. "That's what Kevin would have wanted. I'll do my best with these crutches."

"I'll ask Abby to cover the shop for a little while so Grace and I can pay our respects," Connie said as they were walking to their car.

"Thank you. I appreciate your support. You might even be able to gather some intel on Sally," Ruby said.

Ruby dropped Connie and Grace off at *Just Jewelry* and then returned to her own shop.

"I didn't want to say anything in front of Ruby," Connie said. "But I haven't crossed Tammy off my list of suspects yet."

"I know. I haven't either, but let's keep that between us. There's no need to worry Ruby quite yet."

"We'll keep our eyes open at the wake and see if we can learn anything about Sally. Beyond that, I don't see what else we can do."

The rest of Sunday and Monday went by in a haze of busyness. With so many more customers coming into the store, Connie was on her feet for most of the day, and there was precious little time to make jewelry. She was glad she had taken advantage of the slower months to build her stock.

Abby had graciously agreed to work on Tuesday evening for a few hours so that both Connie and Grace could attend Sally's wake. They wanted to be there to support Ruby but were also hoping, for Amy's sake, that they could learn more about Sally and who might have a motive for her murder.

Connie picked up Grace in front of Palm Paradise, and they arrived at the Anderson-Bradley Funeral Home around 5:00. Since Sally had only lived in Sapphire Beach full-time for a few years, Connie was surprised at how many people were at the wake.

Connie and Grace said a prayer at the casket, then made their way through the receiving line, which included Ruby, Tammy, and two men who Ruby introduced as Tammy's husband, Ray, and their brother, Glen.

"It was very kind of you both to come," Ruby said to Connie and Grace.

"Judging from the crowd, it looks like Sally had a lot of friends in the area," Grace said.

"Many of them are from Community Food Bank," Ruby said. "Apparently, Sally spent more time than I thought volunteering there. I've been listening to some of their stories about Sally. They really loved her there."

Ruby leaned in close to Connie and Grace. "See if you can learn anything," she whispered.

The women nodded, then wandered into the adjoining room where a large group had gathered. Judging from their conversations, they were from the food bank.

A woman with shoulder length auburn hair introduced herself to Connie and Ruby. "Good evening. I'm Pamela, the volunteer coordinator at Community Food Bank. Sally was one of our most faithful volunteers and a good friend."

"I'm so sorry for your loss," Grace said. "We are good friends with Sally's sister-in-law, Ruby."

"Sally was one of our best volunteers. She came faithfully three days a week and was happy to do whatever work we needed. Plus, she organized several successful fundraising dinners. We are devastated that something so horrible could have happened to such a kind and generous woman."

"It doesn't seem fair," Connie said.

As they talked, Connie suddenly got an idea. "Pamela, I've been looking for a place to volunteer. I'd love to stop by the food bank to learn more about your mission."

Pamela's eyes widened, and she pulled a business card from her purse. "I'd be happy to give you a tour."

"How about tomorrow morning?" Connie asked.

Pamela pulled out her phone and checked the calendar app. "Would 11:00 work?"

"Perfect. I'll see you then."

When Pamela was out of earshot, Grace elbowed Connie's arm. "Great idea. Maybe a trip to the food bank will give you some insight into Sally's life."

"That's what I'm hoping," Connie said.

Chapter 5

ON WEDNESDAY MORNING, while on her way to the Palm Paradise parking garage before work, Connie stopped in the lobby with Ginger in tow to check her mail. As she pulled a few bills from her mailbox, Connie was startled by a tap on her shoulder.

"Is that you, Connie?"

It was Brenda, an old friend of Concetta's.

"Brenda!" Connie cried, hugging the woman, whom she hadn't seen since before her aunt passed away. Brenda rented one of the condos in Palm Paradise every year from January through March and during those months, Concetta, Grace, and Brenda used to be inseparable. "I'm so happy to see you."

"I was thrilled to hear that you moved into Concetta's condo after she passed away. I just arrived a couple of weeks ago and have been meaning to stop in. I can't tell you how much I miss Concetta."

As they were talking, the elevator door opened, and Grace came out. She approached the mailboxes but stopped dead in her tracks when she saw Connie and Brenda talking. She paused for an awkward moment, and the tension in the air became tangible.

Connie looked back and forth between the two women, unsure of what to say. They had always been such good friends. What could have happened?

"Hi, Brenda," Grace finally managed.

Brenda smiled nervously at Grace, and Connie couldn't help but notice the sadness in her eyes.

"I'll see you at work, Connie," Grace said abruptly, as she left the lobby without checking her mail.

Brenda appeared crestfallen. "Hopefully, I'll see you soon," she said to Connie, forcing a smile.

Connie heart sank as she watched the elevator door close in front of a heartbroken Brenda.

When Connie arrived at *Just Jewelry*, Grace was brewing a pot of coffee out back. When it was ready, she came out front with two mugs and handed one to Connie. They still had a few minutes before the store was due to open, so they sat at the oak table.

"What on earth was that all about in the lobby?" Connie asked. "You and Brenda were such good friends when Aunt Concetta was alive."

Grace shrugged her shoulders, as if she were unaffected by the encounter. "I guess when times are tough, you find out who your true friends are." But Connie knew Grace better than that.

"What are you talking about, Grace?" Connie asked. "I don't understand."

"It's really quite simple. The three of us were great friends - that is, until Concetta got sick and Brenda disappeared off the face of the earth."

"But Brenda didn't leave because Concetta got sick," Connie said. "She always leaves Sapphire Beach at the end of March. She only rents the condo for three months. Concetta didn't get sick until April and passed away in June."

"True," Grace said. "But I called Brenda and told her about Concetta's illness. I even offered her my guest room so she could come back and help take care of Concetta. But she refused."

"Maybe she had other obligations," Connie said. "Did you ever ask her why?"

A combination of sadness and anger spilled from Grace's words. "There is no excuse for not being there for a friend in her time of extreme need. I don't care what her reason was. She should have been there."

Connie put her arm around Grace's shoulder. "I'm so sorry she hurt you. But knowing my aunt, I doubt she would've held a grudge."

"Maybe not, but that doesn't mean I can't. Brenda should have been there for both of us during that time, and I can't ever forgive her for that."

Connie decided not to press the subject, since it was obviously a sore topic for Grace, and they were getting ready to open the store. So, with a lump in her throat, Connie unlocked the front door and flipped the 'open' sign.

Soon after, a couple came in to browse, followed by another customer, and before she knew it, it was time to head over to Community Food Bank for her appointment with Pamela. Connie absolutely didn't have time to take on a volunteer position at a food bank, so she hoped Pamela wouldn't go in for the hard close and try to get her to sign up on the spot for a shift. This was simply an information gathering appointment as far as Connie was concerned.

Fortunately, Pamela's pitch was low pressure. She gave Connie an informative tour of the warehouse, introducing her to various volunteers and employees along the way. It was an impressive operation. Floor-to-ceiling shelves were stocked with grocery items, which Community Food Bank distributed to partner agencies across the county, including schools, food pantries, and disaster relief agencies.

"We have hundreds of volunteers who do all types of projects for us, including sorting donations, distributing food, running food drives, organizing fundraisers, and general office work. We have one-time volunteer opportunities, or people can commit to regular shifts. We also get many groups who volunteer from local churches, high schools, and from Florida Sands University."

Connie was deeply inspired by the impressive organization, which had so many moving pieces, and she shared with Pamela her experiences in Kenya and with *Feeding the Hungry*. Pamela's tour was so inspiring that Connie had to fight the urge to sign up right then and there to volunteer. The work of helping those who went without enough food was a mission that had always been close to Connie's heart, but there was no way she could fit another activity into her already-hectic schedule. Especially if she kept getting sucked into murder investigations.

The tour ended in the volunteer break room, where Pamela offered Connie a cup of coffee. Fortunately, there was nobody else in there, so Connie accepted the coffee and took the opportunity to direct the conversation toward Sally.

"I'm so sorry that you lost your friend and star volunteer in such a senseless tragedy," Connie said. "I'm sure that Sally is going to be hard to replace."

"Thank you. Sally was a one-of-a-kind volunteer. People serve for all sorts of reasons, but Sally did it to honor her deceased husband, Kevin. She often talked about how he had hoped to retire early from his career as a lawyer to spend his time volunteering, and she regretted never giving him the opportunity."

"It seems like Sally was trying to make up for the good he could have done," Connie said.

"That's exactly what she used to say." Pamela chuckled. "I heard that it took a while for her to settle on Community Food Bank as the place she would do most of her volunteering. Apparently, she used to show up regularly for a Saturday build at a Habitat for Humanity site until she realized that construction was not her gift. Sally originally worked with Habitat, because that's the work Kevin would have done. Fortunately, her friends managed to convince her that her skill set was elsewhere and that she should contribute according to her own abilities. We were thrilled she gave us a try."

"What an inspiring story," Connie said.

"Sally's favorite project was helping us with fundraising. When she first started, she offered to host a fundraising dinner. She got the food and venue at a deep discount, organized volunteers to decorate and act as waiters and waitresses - the whole nine yards. It was so successful that she organized two dinners every year. As a result, donations were at an all-time high. She also came regularly to sort food and help with administrative projects." Pamela shook her head. "Sally was taken much too young. She should have had many more years on this earth."

"And many more years helping those in need," Connie added. "I hope the police are able to bring her killer to justice."

Pamela looked away and swallowed hard.

Was that a reaction to grief, Connie wondered, *or did Pamela know something?*

Connie tried to reestablish eye contact. "It's hard to imagine such a kind and generous woman having any enemies. Can you think of anyone who might have wanted to harm Sally?"

Pamela's eyes grew moist. "It's probably nothing. The police were here earlier this week, and I answered all their questions."

"Is there something you didn't tell them?"

"It's not my place to go accusing people of murder," Pamela said.

Connie tried another approach. "Pamela, I'm not a detective, but I have helped solve some mysteries in the past. If you have any information, I'd be happy to look into it discreetly." Connie looked directly at Pamela. "I understand the importance of the work you do here, and I also understand that you don't want any unnecessary negative press that would affect donations."

"A drop in donations could mean that hungry children won't get their next meal," Pamela said.

Connie's heart went out to Pamela. She was in a difficult spot. She had to choose the life-saving mission of the food bank or potentially helping to put a murderer behind bars. "I understand your fears. You can trust me to be discreet. If there is a killer among you, he or she has to be held accountable."

Pamela stuck her head out the doorway and glanced around the hallway. Then she closed the door and sat back down across from Connie. "You're right. Sally deserves justice. I'm trusting you to handle this information with caution. In the couple of months before Sally's death, there was obvious tension growing between Kyle Beckett, Chief Financial Officer of the food bank, and Sally."

"If Sally was a model volunteer who raised so much money for the organization, where did the tension come from?"

Sally shrugged her shoulders. "I wish I knew. One day Sally was Kyle's favorite volunteer. He would often recruit her to do administrative projects for him, especially since his administrative assistant was on maternity leave, and the temps he had were unreliable. She had worked as an executive assistant at various companies before she married Kevin, so she had strong office skills. However, a couple of months ago Sally was sorting food and Kyle came over to borrow her for a project. He said he would need her for a few hours, but a half hour later, her sent her back to the sorting area. She was unable to concentrate and barely talked to anyone for the rest of her shift. After that day, Kyle never requested her help again. In fact, there was clearly tension in the air whenever the two of them were in the same room."

"Do you have *any* idea what might have happened?"

"At first, I shrugged it off, thinking maybe it was an attraction gone bad. Kyle can be a bit of a flirt, so I thought maybe he tried something, and she rejected him."

"I guess that could explain it," Connie said.

"But the more I think about it, the less sense that theory makes. Sally would have told me if that had happened. We were friends. Whatever happened was something she was afraid to tell me about. Of course, now, I wish I had pressed her more. I just figured she'd tell me when she was ready."

Connie thanked Pamela for her time and politely took some information on becoming a volunteer. "If you can figure out who killed Sally," Pamela said, "that would be the best volunteer contribution you could make to our organization."

When Connie returned to *Just Jewelry,* Grace was scrambling to serve a wave of customers, so Connie jumped right into action. Around lunchtime, when things slowed down, Connie texted Ruby and invited her over. When Ruby arrived, Connie caught Grace and Ruby up on her conversation with Pamela, including the part about Sally choosing to spend her time volunteering in honor of Kevin.

"I had no idea Sally had regrets about not letting Kevin retire early," Ruby said. "Maybe I should have cut her some slack."

"Well, the best way we can honor her now is to help put her killer behind bars," Grace said. "I wonder what caused the friction between Sally and Kyle?"

"I don't know," Connie said. "And I can't think of any excuse to arrange a meeting with Kyle to try to find out."

"Meeting with Pamela was one thing," Grace said. "She's the volunteer coordinator. But we have no reason to meet with the Chief Financial Officer. Even if we pretended that we wanted to make a donation, he would probably refer us to someone on the development staff."

"We might not need to talk with Kyle," Ruby said. "I might have a source who can give us some information."

"Have you been holding out on us?" Grace asked playfully.

Ruby waved her hand at Grace. "Of course not. I just forgot about Sally's best friend, Denise. We talked at the wake and exchanged phone numbers. She was visibly disturbed by what happened to Sally, so I want to check in on her, anyway. I can kill two birds with one stone by checking on Denise, and if you both come, you can help me gather some more intel."

"Sounds like a good next step," Connie said.

"I'll try to arrange a visit for the weekend when you have more coverage at *Just Jewelry*," Ruby said.

Chapter 6

THURSDAY WENT by in a haze. Connie worked alone most of the day, until Abby arrived at 4:30. Her Thursday evening jewelry-making class was growing with the influx of snowbirds, so she decided to add a Saturday morning class beginning in March.

On Friday afternoon, Ruby texted to confirm their visit with Sally's friend, Denise, for the following afternoon at 4:30, which was perfect. She would easily be able to sneak away for a while, since Abby would be working.

When Abby arrived on Saturday afternoon, Connie and Ruby dropped off Ginger at Palm Paradise and picked up Grace on their way to Denise's home. Denise's condominium was just down the street from Palm Paradise, so they arrived right on time. Denise buzzed them in through the intercom in the foyer outside the lobby, and they took the elevator to the fourth floor. The building was similar to Palm Paradise, except the décor was a bit more rustic. When they entered Denise's apartment, the layout was different, but the expansive view of the Gulf of Mexico was identical to Connie's.

Denise led them to the balcony, then brought out four steaming mugs of tea on a tray, along with some macaroons that Ruby brought.

"How are you doing?" Ruby asked Denise, after introducing her to Connie and Grace. "I've been concerned about you since we talked at the wake."

Denise shrugged. "I'm taking it one day at a time. I keep expecting Sally to call me at any moment. And then I remember…" Her eyes moistened.

Grace patted Denise's hand. "I'm so sorry that you lost your best friend. My best friend passed away a year-and-a-half ago, and not a day goes by that I don't miss her."

Connie smiled warmly at Grace. There were some things you never got over. You just had to do your best to move forward.

"I keep telling myself that I was blessed to have her in my life, even if only for a short time, but I can't help but focus on the loss," Denise said. "She was only fifty-eight years old. What kind of monster would have taken her life so soon?"

"I wish I knew," Ruby said, shaking her head. "We've been asking ourselves the same question since it happened last Friday night. I know I wasn't always the best sister-in-law, but I'm trying to do right by Sally now. I've asked Connie to do some investigating to help bring her killer to justice. Connie has a good track record helping the police."

Denise put her hand on Ruby's. "Sally understood why it was difficult for you and your family to be around her. Her biggest regret in life was not allowing Kevin to retire early like he wanted. She always wondered if he still would have had his heart attack if he had left the stress of his high-powered job."

"I wish I had known while she was still alive that Sally felt that way," Ruby said.

Judging from the guilty expression on Grace's face, Connie guessed that she was thinking about her own relationship with Brenda. Connie shot her an I-told-you-so glance, which Grace intentionally avoided.

"The reason we came over with Ruby," Grace said, "was to see if you knew anything that might shed some light on Sally's untimely death."

"I wish I could help you, but as I told the police, I have no idea who would have done this to her."

"It's possible you know more than you think," Connie said. "Pamela, from Community Food Bank, said there was some tension between Sally and Kyle, the CFO. Did she ever mention this to you?"

Denise thought for a moment. "She never mentioned anything about Kyle, but come to think of it, in the past couple of months, she seemed less enthusiastic about volunteering at the food bank. Going there used to be the highlight of her week, but the last time we had dinner, she said she was thinking of finding a new place to volunteer."

Ruby looked optimistic. "It sounds like Sally had a significant problem with Kyle. It's worth looking into."

"There's one more thing we wanted to ask you," Connie said. "Tammy mentioned that Sally was seeing someone. Can you tell us anything about him?"

"You must mean Tim. Sally dated him for a few months, but her heart wasn't in it. Some of our friends kept insisting she get back into the dating scene. She was still young, and there are plenty of great guys in Sapphire Beach. One of our friends introduced her to Tim. I think she went out with him to get everyone off her back, but she was never really into the relationship. Besides, Tim had a jealous ex-girlfriend who didn't hesitate to make her intentions with Tim clear to Sally. To her, it just wasn't worth dealing with."

"Wow," Ruby said. "Sally had a lot going on between her boyfriend drama and the food bank drama."

"I guess she did," Denise said. "She broke it off with Tim recently, though."

"That's understandable," Ruby said.

"Have you talked to the woman who found the body?" Denise asked. "Sally called me the day she passed away and told me she was meeting with a woman who claimed to be Kevin's biological daughter. She could have been some sort of psycho for all we know."

Ruby's shoulders stiffened. "I met Amy, and I have no doubt that she's innocent."

"How can you be so certain?" Denise asked. "How many times did you meet her?"

"Just once, but we talked many times on the phone. She was a Peace Corps volunteer and a teacher – not the type that goes around killing people they don't even know."

"Good people turn bad all the time. Just promise me you won't rule her out just because she claims to be Kevin's daughter."

Ruby was getting upset, so Connie chimed in. "We promise to keep an open mind, but it sounds like the police are already looking into that possibility. We just want to be sure they consider every angle."

Connie's reassurance seemed to help, because Ruby relaxed her shoulders and got the conversation back on track. "Would you by chance have any contact information for Tim?" Ruby asked. "I'd really like to talk to him."

"I think I might," Denise said. She went inside the house and grabbed her phone off the coffee table. "He's also a handyman and did some work in my house." Denise rattled off the number, and Ruby programmed it into her phone.

Since Connie and Ruby had to get back to work, the women only visited for a few more minutes, just long enough to cheer up Denise and for Ruby to assure her that if she felt depressed and wanted to talk, all she had to do was call.

Connie returned to *Just Jewelry* to work with Abby, who still hadn't heard anything about her graduate school application.

"A few of my friends have received acceptance letters from other schools," Abby said when Connie inquired, "so the more time goes by, the more nervous I get."

"They'd be crazy not to accept you, Abby."

On Sunday morning, Connie spotted Grace at the 7:00 Mass, which was unusual, since Grace normally went to the 9:00 Mass.

Sliding into the pew next to Grace, Connie whispered, "Why such an early start?"

Grace wore a mischievous expression.

"Don't be mad," she said.

"Umm, okay…Why would I be mad?"

"Palm Paradise is running a kayaking excursion this morning at 9:00."

"Say no more," Connie said, giving her friend a one-armed hug. "Take the day off and enjoy the kayaking excursion. You have more than earned it."

Grace chuckled. "I'm not going on the excursion. *You* are."

Connie shot her a confused look.

"Since you haven't been able to take a day off since Christmas, and you're doing so much work to help Ruby, I thought you needed a change of pace for a couple of hours."

"You're too much, Grace."

"I think it's meant to be. On Friday afternoon, I ran into Jessica in the lobby. She was talking up the excursion, because there still were a few slots left. Since I've gone in the past, she tried to encourage me to sign up. But instead I signed *you* up." Jessica was the management company's employee who held office hours at Palm Paradise.

Connie had to admit, a couple of hours on the water sounded like a great way to spend the morning.

"I hope you're not mad," Grace said. "But I already paid for your kayak rental so you wouldn't have to borrow one and lug it to the site. She handed Connie a slip of paper with an address. All you have to do is show up at this kayak rental place. It right on the Matlacha Pass Aquatic Preserve. Jessica will be there, too. It's only two hours. You'll be back in the shop before lunch."

The opening procession was about to start, so there wasn't time to protest. And the idea of a couple of hours outdoors sounded wonderful. "Thank you, Grace. That was really thoughtful. Are you sure you don't mind being alone in the store for a couple of hours?"

"No problem at all. By the time things start to get busy, you'll be back."

After Mass, Connie stopped by Palm Paradise to change and left behind a confused Ginger, who was used to coming to work with Connie. "I'll be back in a couple of hours to take you to the shop, sweet girl."

Connie arrived at the aquatic preserve a few minutes early so she could get situated with her kayak.

Jessica laughed when she saw her. "I hope you don't mind that Grace signed you up without your permission," she said. "I was tempted to call you to make sure it was okay, but Grace insisted on surprising you."

"That's okay. It was a pleasant surprise," Connie said. "It's been a busy couple of months, and I haven't had time to enjoy the outdoors like I promised myself I would when I moved to Florida."

Once everyone arrived, which turned out to be a group of about twenty participants, they strapped on their life jackets, launched their kayaks, and began paddling through the Matlacha Pass with their guide, Joe, leading them.

Joe went out of his way to put at ease the newbie kayakers while pointing out various subtropical vegetation as they paddled along through mangrove mazes and tree canopies. As they explored the estuary, Connie spotted sea turtles, an array of subtropical birds, and even a few manatees.

The more distance Connie put between herself and the shop, as well as the murder investigation, the clearer her head felt. As much as she loved owning a jewelry shop, a couple of hours off was just what the doctor ordered. A doctor named Grace, apparently.

Connie chatted with a few of the other participants as they glided through the waterway, and while she was talking with Jessica, Connie spotted Brenda a short distance ahead. When Connie and Jessica were finished catching up, Connie pulled up her kayak alongside Brenda, who was paddling alone.

Brenda smiled nervously, so Connie did her best to set her at ease. "It's wonderful to see you here, Brenda. The preserve is breathtaking."

"It really is," Brenda said. "Nature has a way of soothing the soul."

Connie had a feeling Brenda's soul needed soothing because of the way Grace treated her in the lobby the other day.

"I'm sorry things are tense between you and Grace," Connie said.

"I don't blame Grace for being angry with me," Brenda said. "I should have returned to Sapphire Beach when Concetta got sick and been there for her final months. I'll always regret that decision. But...I just couldn't face it."

"It was a hard time," Connie said. "But I want to thank you for your friendship toward my aunt over the years. She loved you very much."

Brenda wiped a tear with the back of her hand. "Being Concetta's friend was the easiest thing in the world. It was losing her that I couldn't bear."

They paddled for a couple of minutes without talking, then Brenda broke the silence.

"Less than a year before Concetta got sick, my sister died from colon cancer, the same cancer that Concetta had. I never talk about it much with my friends in Sapphire Beach, because it was too difficult. They knew my sister died of cancer, but I never shared any of the details. They respected my privacy and didn't press me to talk about it, which I appreciated. I wanted to be there for Concetta, but I just couldn't go through it again, especially so soon after losing my sister."

"I'm so sorry for your loss, Brenda, but Grace should know about this."

"I don't think so, Connie. As I said, I should have been there for my friends, and I wasn't. I don't think my reasons are important."

"Grace might disagree if she knew the truth," Connie said. "You should at least give her a chance."

Brenda appeared to be contemplating Connie's suggestion, so she gave her some space to reflect and enjoy the peaceful surroundings of the aquatic preserve.

When they finished their paddle, vans from the rental company were waiting to transport the group, along with their kayaks, back to where they started.

Chapter 7

AFTER CONNIE'S KAYAKING expedition, she swung by her condo to pick up Ginger and change, then stopped at Grace's favorite sandwich shop to buy lunch as a thank you for sending her on the trip. All the paddling had worked up an appetite, and Connie's stiff shoulders were already reminding her that it had been too long since her last adventure on the water. She ordered a thick turkey club sandwich with bacon to load up on protein and got Grace her favorite lunch – a brie sandwich with green apple and Dijon mustard on a French baguette.

The morning in the sunshine and fresh air brought Connie a burst of energy that lasted throughout the afternoon.

Around 5:00, Ruby stopped in.

"You're getting faster on those crutches," Abby said.

"Thanks, honey. My shoulders have never been so strong. The doctor said I should be off them in another couple of weeks."

"Watch out, world," Connie teased.

"I plan to take it nice and slow after my latest mishap," Ruby said. "I can't stay long, but I wanted to tell you that I called Tim, Sally's ex-boyfriend, and asked if we could talk. He's going to be downtown running some errands tomorrow morning and said he'd come to my shop. I was hoping you could break away for a little while so we could talk to him together."

"Grace will be here in the morning, so it shouldn't be a problem," Connie said.

"Perfect. I'll see you then."

Business was slower on Sunday evenings, so Connie and Abby created some social media advertising campaigns and flyers for their new Saturday morning jewelry-making class. Since Abby worked Thursday through Sunday evenings, and Grace worked until 1:00 every day except Tuesdays and Thursdays, Connie would have assistance in the store during both her Thursday evening and Saturday morning classes, which meant she would be able to give her students her full attention.

On Monday morning, Ruby brought Tim to *Just Jewelry* as planned. Connie, Ruby, and Tim went to the closest coffee shop, so Ruby wouldn't have to go too far on her crutches, and took their beverages to an outdoor table.

"Ruby explained that you were hoping I could provide some information about Sally that might explain what happened to her, but I don't think I can be of much help," Tim said. "Sally and I dated off and on for about six months, and to be honest, it was mostly off. Things never got serious between us. Sally was always too busy with her volunteering for a relationship, but I think that was just an excuse. Although it had been four years since her husband passed away, if you ask me, she still wasn't ready to move on. And I doubt she ever would have been."

"Kevin was a tough act to follow," Ruby said with a faraway expression.

Tim smiled graciously. "I'm sure he was. And that's why we never really got close. We were more like dinner companions. I kept hoping she would eventually want more if I was patient, but it just never happened. She was looking for a friend more than anything else."

"One of Sally's friends mentioned that you had an ex-girlfriend who was quite jealous of Sally," Connie said. "We were hoping you could tell us more about her. Did she have a temper?"

"What are you implying?" Tim asked, furrowing his brow.

"Please understand, we don't mean any offense," Connie said. "We are just exploring every possibility. Do you have any way of knowing where she was the night Sally was killed?"

Tim looked deeply offended. "I understand your situation, but there is no way Patsy would ever kill anyone. She may not have an alibi, but she's not the violent type. In fact, Patsy and I just decided to give it another shot. Obviously, I wouldn't be dating anyone I thought was a killer," Tim said, as if his revelation definitively ended that possibility.

"You're seeing each other again?" Connie asked.

"As a matter of fact, we just started dating again last week. Look, you seem sincere and I'm very sorry for your loss, so I'll tell you what I told the police. I would look at a woman named Gloria. She and her husband, Don, live next door to Sally."

"Was there trouble between them?" Connie asked.

"Last summer, Sally went to visit a friend in Wisconsin for a month. When she returned, Don had built a garage that infringed on Sally's property line, and Sally threatened to report them to the Building Department."

"So, Gloria and Don waited until Sally was out of town to build the structure?" Ruby asked.

"That's what Sally thought. They claimed it was just a coincidence, but either way, Sally was furious when she got home. I was there when Sally confronted Gloria, and it wasn't pretty."

The women thanked Tim for his time and returned to *Just Jewelry* to fill Grace in on their conversation.

"So, is Patsy still on your list of suspects?" Grace asked.

"At this stage, I would say so," Connie said. "She apparently doesn't have an alibi, and we only have Tim's opinion that she's innocent."

"And he is biased," Ruby said.

"Tim said he and Patsy started dating again last week, which would have been just after Sally died," Connie said.

"That's some coincidence," Grace said. "Maybe Patsy's plan to kill Sally and get Tim back was successful."

"Patsy could have believed that, as long as Tim was hoping for more with Sally, she didn't stand a chance with him," Connie said. "Tim said himself that he hoped if he was patient, Sally might change her mind."

Ruby stared blankly into the distance. "I should have been kinder to Sally after my brother died. After all, she was hurting every bit as much as I was. I should have supported her during the hard times instead of blaming her. Now I am even more determined to see her killer behind bars – not just to help Amy but also to ensure that justice is served for Sally, as well."

"By the way, how is Amy doing?" Connie asked.

Ruby shook her head back and forth. "Not great, I'm afraid. In the past month, not only did she learn that her father was no longer alive, she walked into a murder scene and is accused of killing his widow.

76

Amy's mother wants her to break off contact with me, but Amy is insisting on staying in touch."

"We'll keep investigating, but I hope the police are making more progress than we are," Connie said.

"My money is on you, Connie," Ruby said. "Grace is always bragging about your sleuthing skills. She says that your analytical mind and sense of justice make you a great amateur detective."

Connie gave Grace a confused look. "I didn't know you were proud. You are always urging me to stay out of these things."

"Oh, I'm just worried about your safety. But I'm really proud of how many killers have been put behind bars since you moved to Sapphire Beach."

"Speaking of putting killers behind bars, maybe we should meet up with Amy to catch her up on the case and lend some moral support. It must be a tough time for her."

"That's a fabulous idea," Ruby said. "What about this evening?"

"I'm alone in the store tonight, so I wouldn't be able to get together until after 9:00. Is that too late?" Connie asked.

Ruby and Grace both agreed that would work, so Ruby called Amy, who was happy for the chance to get together. Connie offered her condo as a meeting place for some privacy, and Grace promised to bring dessert.

That evening, Connie left *Just Jewelry* right at 9:00 and drove the one-mile commute home to Palm Paradise just in time to receive her company.

Grace was the first to arrive, since she lived right next door, so they set the pastries she brought, along with two bottles of wine, one red and one white, on the dining room table. Shortly after, Ruby and Amy arrived.

Light gray circles, which weren't there the first time Connie met Amy, appeared beneath Amy's eyes.

"How are you doing?" Connie asked as she passed a plate of pastries Amy's way.

Amy selected an eclair and shrugged while she placed it on her plate. "I've been better. I know I'm not guilty, so I keep telling myself that the truth will eventually come out. I want to thank the three of you for your support though all this. Ruby tells me you've been investigating."

"We're family," Ruby said. "We're in this together."

"And any family of Ruby's is our friend," Grace said.

"We don't know that much yet, but we've managed to talk to a few people and acquire a list of suspects – or at least people with a motive and no alibi," Connie said

"That sounds like a good start. Who's on your list so far?" Amy asked.

"First, we learned that Sally volunteers at a local food bank, and there is was major tension between Sally and the CFO, Kyle," Connie said. "According to the volunteer director, who was also friends with Sally, there was some type of falling out between the two of them, but nobody knows what happened."

"And according to Denise, who was a close friend of Sally's," Grace said, "she was planning to quit the food bank and find a new place to volunteer."

"Another suspect is Sally's neighbor, Gloria, and her husband, Don," Connie said. "We learned that they built a garage too close to the property line dividing their home from Sally's, and Sally wanted them to take it down, because it violated code. We haven't had a chance to talk to them yet, but they are next on our list."

"That could be a motive," Amy said. "Especially if there have been other issues between them. Anybody else?"

Connie decided not to mention Tammy. There was no point in upsetting Ruby or Amy when they had other leads to work on for now. She didn't think Ruby could handle losing her sister or that Amy should be worrying about whether one of her aunts is a killer, on top of everything else they were dealing with. If the other leads turned out to be dead ends, Connie would focus more energy on Tammy.

"One more," Connie said. "Sally dated a man named Tim for few months who had a jealous ex-girlfriend, Patsy. It seems that Tim and Patsy got back together right after Sally died."

"So, you're thinking she might have killed Sally to eliminate the competition?"

"It's a possibility that I haven't ruled out yet. I'd like to talk to Kyle and Gloria to try to learn more, but I'm not sure how to arrange that. We're not the police, so nobody has to talk to us. And we don't want to just show up at their door. We want to be discreet."

They sat in silence as they sipped their wine and enjoyed their pastries, each lost in her own thoughts.

Suddenly, Grace pushed her empty dish away. "I have an idea. Hold on one second," she said, running out the front door of Connie's apartment.

A few minutes later, Grace returned holding a flyer that she received in the mail. "I'm on the mailing list for Community Food Bank, and I happen to know that this Wednesday they need volunteers to sort a large donation they received. The flyer says they are looking for twenty-five volunteers to join their staff from 10:00 AM to Noon. I'll bet Kyle will be there. I work on Wednesdays, anyway, so I can cover the store if you guys want to go."

"I could take the time off, too," Ruby said. "My employees have everything under control. Nobody would miss me."

"Can you volunteer with your sprained ankle?" Connie asked.

"It's getting better every day," Ruby said. "Besides, I'm sure I can sit while I work."

"I guess it's worth a try," Connie said.

"I wish I could come, but I have to work," Amy said.

"No worries," Connie said. "We've got this covered."

Chapter 8

THE NEXT DAY was so hectic that Connie didn't have a spare minute to focus on anything except work. She was used to handling the store alone, but Tuesday was the only day she was alone from opening to closing, so it made for a long day.

Fortunately, Ruby stopped in to let Connie know that she registered them both to volunteer at the food bank on Wednesday, so Connie enlisted Ruby to watch the shop while she took Ginger for a much-needed walk. During the slow summer months, Connie could close the store for a few minutes but during the busy season, that would likely mean losing business.

On Wednesday morning, after briefly working with Grace at *Just Jewelry*, Connie and Ruby headed over to Community Food Bank for their volunteer commitment and with the intention to gather additional intel.

Pamela greeted them warmly and introduced them to the other volunteers, most of whom seemed to know one another. Pamela made it a point to announce to the group of about twenty volunteers that Ruby was Sally's sister-in-law.

Pamela divided the volunteers into groups and instructed them on sorting the boxes of donations into bags for individual families. They were to be given away at one of the food bank's mobile food pantries. Fortunately, there were plenty of stools for Ruby to use while she sorted grocery items.

As Connie and Ruby sorted grocery items at a stainless steel workstation, Connie glanced around the room, contemplating her next move. The volunteers were mostly women, except for a few older men, so it didn't look like Kyle was there. She hoped he would stop by later.

A few of the volunteers came over to offer their condolences and share stories about working with Sally. Sally must have considered her fellow volunteers as friends, because apparently, she had even talked with some of them about Amy and the coffee meeting they were supposed to have the day Sally was killed. Ruby assured them that there was no way Amy would hurt anyone and told them how anxious she was for the real killer to be discovered, so that Amy could put this nightmare behind her.

One particular woman was especially kind. "My name is Deidra," she said, after taking a few boxes of sorted non-perishables and moving them to another workstation, where a different group was bagging the items. "I just wanted you to know how sorry we all were to hear about what happened to Sally. I know I speak on behalf of all the volunteers who worked with her when I say that she will be sorely missed."

"Thank you," Ruby said. "It's very kind of you to say."

"Say, Pamela introduced you as Sally's sister-in-law," Deidra said. "Was Sally's late husband Kevin your brother?"

Ruby smiled at the mention of Kevin's name. "Yes, as a matter of fact he was. Did you know him?"

"I never had the pleasure of meeting him directly," Deidra said. "But Sally talked about him so much that I felt like I knew him. She would often talk about how Kevin was the inspiration for all the volunteer work she did."

Ruby swallowed hard. "I know the loss of my brother was devastating to her, but I have to be honest, I didn't realize how much time she spent honoring his memory."

"I volunteered with her three days a week, and I don't think a day went by when she didn't bring him up at least once. Well, I'd better return to my station," Deidra said. "I just wanted to offer my condolences."

When Connie and Ruby returned to their sorting duties, Ruby's eyes were moist. "I think maybe God is trying to tell me something"

Connie stopped working. "What do you mean?"

"In the past couple of weeks, several people have gone out of their way to tell me how much Kevin meant to Sally. If her actions did contribute to Kevin's heart attack, she was clearly very sorry. She may have made some decisions that weren't in his best interest, but I know she never would have intentionally hurt my brother. Maybe it's time to forgive and let go, once and for all."

Connie squeezed Ruby's forearm. "If she was responsible, even partly, she was obviously sorry and did everything she could to make up for it."

Connie and Ruby continued working in silence, but after a few minutes Connie suddenly stopped. "Do you think you could tell that to Grace?"

"I guess so," Ruby said. "Why?"

Connie told Ruby about the grudge Grace held against Brenda for not being present during Concetta's illness, and how Grace, Concetta, and Brenda used to be the best of friends. She also explained what Brenda told her during the kayaking expedition about her sister dying of colon cancer shortly before. "I think it would help both Grace and Brenda if the two could make peace, and you just might be able to nudge her in that direction."

Ruby nodded. "I see what you mean. I'll try to talk to her."

Their two-hour shift was quickly drawing to a close, and so far, the morning hadn't been as productive as Connie had hoped.

With about a half hour to go, a young man who looked to be in his early twenties, entered the room where they were working and began chatting with some of the volunteers.

After talking to one of the groups, the young man looked over at Connie and Ruby with a scowl on his face.

Connie gently elbowed Ruby to draw her attention toward the young man.

"It can't be Kyle," Ruby said. "He's much too young."

"I know, but he was staring daggers at us. I wonder who he could be."

They didn't have to wonder for long. The young man plastered a friendly smile on his face and came over to introduce himself.

"My name is Jack Beckett," he said. "My father works for the food bank, and I like to help out when I can."

"Your father must be Kyle Beckett then," Connie said. "It's nice to meet you, Jack. I'm Connie, and this is Ruby."

Jack studied Connie for a moment. He looked surprised that Connie knew who his father was.

"It's great to meet you," Jack said. "I hear that you learned about our organization through Sally

Boyd. We were so sorry to hear about what happened to her. She will be missed."

Jack seemed pleasant enough, but why had he scowled at them when he was talking to the other volunteer?

"Thank you," Connie said. "Sally certainly loved Community Food Bank. I understand she would often assist your father with special projects."

Jack furrowed his brow. "I suppose she did, but there's nothing special about that. All the regulars assist my dad from time to time. People are only too happy to help him, because everyone is aware of the important work he does for the community. In fact, I think my father only met Sally once or twice. She wasn't that great at office projects, so he preferred to use her skills for other things."

Connie distinctly remembered Pamela saying that Sally used to be an executive assistant before she married Kevin.

"I'm sure your father is very faithful to the food bank's mission," Ruby said.

"Absolutely," Connie said. "There's so much corruption in the news these days, it's refreshing to hear about people with honesty and integrity." Connie maintained eye contact with Jack.

Jack looked as if Connie had punched him in the stomach. He took a deep breath and flashed them one of the phoniest smiles Connie had ever seen.

"Yes, my father is an inspiration to many people, and he will be for many years to come," Jack said. Then he left the room.

"That's strange," Pamela said, after Jack left. "He said he would stay and help until the end."

"I guess something came up," Connie said, mentally adding Jack to her suspect list.

Chapter 9

THE REST OF WEDNESDAY and Thursday were uneventful. As usual, on Thursday evening, Connie's jewelry-making class gathered. This week, they created bracelets with diamond-like beads surrounding a snowflake charm.

Connie had been surprised at the group's winter-themed choice, but as one woman put it, "Snow is beautiful, as long as you don't have to shovel out your car."

A few minutes before Connie and Grace opened the store on Friday morning, Ruby popped in. "Detective Miller called yesterday to tell me that Sally's home was no longer a crime scene. I am free to enter the house and start preparing it to be sold."

"That sounds like a daunting task, especially with a sprained ankle," Grace said. "Are your brother and sister going to help you?"

"It looks like the responsibility has fallen on my shoulders. Sally named me as the executor to her will, since she had no living blood relatives, and I was Kevin's closest sister. After Kevin died, she asked me if I would do it and I agreed, but then we grew apart in the years after Kevin's death, so I was surprised that she never changed it. I could ask Tammy and Glen for help, but I thought I'd go through Sally's belongings myself in case there are any clues pointing to her killer."

"That's too much work for one person, especially with your ankle," Grace said. "We can do it together. If nothing else, I can lend you some moral support."

"I'd be happy to come, too," Connie said. "Just say the word. And Elyse is a fantastic realtor. I can put the two of you in touch when you're ready."

"I'll take the realtor referral," Ruby said. "But the two of you are already doing so much for me. I couldn't ask you to help me clean out her house. Besides, this sprained ankle is only temporary. It feels better every day."

"You *didn't* ask," Grace said. "We volunteered."

"Thank you," Ruby said reluctantly. "I suppose I could use the help."

They agreed to head over to Sally's late that afternoon after Abby arrived.

"There's something I learned this morning when I was talking to Sally's lawyer that I think you should know," Ruby said. "It seems that Sally changed her will three years ago to include a sizeable donation to Community Food Bank, but a few weeks before she died, she amended her will again. She simply left a sum of money to be donated to a worthy organization of my choosing."

"It sounds like she no longer trusted the food bank," Connie said. "I wish I knew what she discovered in Kyle's office."

Connie texted Elyse about the potential listing, and Elyse agreed to meet them at Sally's house to take a preliminary look.

Elyse, Grace, and Ruby were already there by the time Connie arrived, after she dropped Ginger off at the condo. Sally's home was a single-family dwelling located on a side street between downtown and the Sapphire Beach State Park. On one side of the house was a hallway that led to three good-sized bedrooms and two newly renovated bathrooms. Sally had converted one of the spare bedrooms into a craft room, and the other was set up as a guest room. On the other side was a palatial master bedroom suite located off the living room.

Just past the double sliding doors was a large screened-in lanai with a small swimming pool and built-in hot tub, and on the right was an outdoor kitchen with granite countertops and a stainless steel grill.

As they were discussing a plan of action, Ruby's gaze settled on the area in the living room where Amy had described finding Sally's body. Fortunately, Ruby had called in a cleaning company that Josh had recommended, which specialized in tough cleanups, so the pool of blood was no longer there.

Connie placed her hand on Ruby's shoulder. "Try not to think about it."

Ruby gave Elyse a tour of the house, and they discussed a listing price. While Ruby was telling Elyse about the garage situation next door, they were distracted by the loud grinding sound of the garage door opening next door.

Connie peeked out the window. "That must be Gloria's house. The garage is practically touching the other side of the fence."

Ruby stood behind Connie and peered over her shoulder. "It looks like she is just getting home. We need to find a way to talk to her."

Connie opened a few of the kitchen cabinets and pulled out a serving dish. "I have an idea," she said, walking toward the front door. "Follow my lead."

Connie marched next door to Gloria's house, followed by Grace, Elyse and lastly, Ruby on her crutches. She rang the doorbell, and a woman with shoulder length grey hair and small, dark eyes appeared behind the door.

"May I help you?" she asked, sounding more interested in getting rid of them than being of assistance.

Ruby took the lead. "My name is Ruby Boyd. Sally Boyd was my sister-in-law. I'm sure you heard the tragic news about her death."

Gloria suddenly changed her expression to appear sympathetic. "Oh, yes, poor Sally. Such a tragedy.

We always thought we lived in a safe neighborhood, and then something like this happens. My name is Gloria. I wish I could invite you in, but I just stopped home for a couple of minutes before heading out again. But please accept my condolences for your loss."

"We won't take much of your time," Connie said. "We just came across this serving dish at Sally's house. Ruby didn't recognize it, so we thought it might belong to you." She held up the dish for Gloria to see.

A middle-aged man with thinning brown hair appeared in the doorway behind Gloria. He introduced himself as Gloria's husband, Don.

Gloria examined the serving platter. "Oh, yes, that's mine," she said, snatching the dish from Connie's hands. "Thank you for returning it. Now if you'll excuse me, I really must go."

But before Gloria could close the door, Ruby put one of her crutches in the doorway to stop it from closing. "We were just wondering if you were home when Sally was murdered, and if so, if you saw anything."

"Of course we didn't see anything, or we would have told the police when they came by to ask us the same question. I was here with my husband all afternoon, and we didn't see or hear anything."

Ruby removed her crutch from the doorway.

"One more thing," Elyse said before Gloria could close the door. "I'm a realtor, and I'll be listing Sally's home." She handed Gloria a business card, which she passed to Don. "I noticed that your garage is quite close to Sally's property line. Are you able to produce a permit for it?"

Anger flashed in Gloria's eyes. "I don't have time to discuss business right now. I really must go. Thank you for returning the platter."

Before they could say anything else, the door slammed in their faces.

The three women stood looking at one another in complete surprise before returning to Sally's house.

"I can't believe she actually took the platter," Connie said, finally breaking their stunned silence. "I only meant to use it as an excuse to stop over. I never imagined she'd *actually* take it."

"I guess she seized the opportunity to take one last jab at Sally," Ruby said.

"Well, that wasn't very productive," Connie said. "We might as well get to work."

The women developed a rhythm as they sorted through Sally's belongings. Connie and Grace brought each item to Ruby, who was seated on the couch to avoid putting pressure on her ankle, and Ruby directed them to put it in one of three piles – keep, donate, or throw away.

They made quick work of bagging all Sally's clothes to donate them to a thrift shop. Ruby placed Sally's jewelry in a small tote bag to be distributed among the family as mementos, since much of her jewelry had been purchased by Kevin as gifts over the years.

"Sally really scaled down her possessions after Kevin passed away," Ruby said. "Back home in Wisconsin, she had a large walk-in closet filled designer clothes, shoes, and handbags."

Once the clothes were bagged, Connie loaded them into her car so she could bring them to the thrift shop the following morning.

Next, Connie and Grace helped Ruby set aside any sentimental items that belonged to Sally. They boxed up photo albums, framed pictures, and other personal items so Connie could load them in Ruby's car.

"After the dust settles from this investigation, I want to give everyone in my family some of these items. There are a lot of happy memories in these boxes," Ruby said. She tapped one of the boxes filled with photos. "There are tons of photos of Kevin in here. I'd also like to make some copies for Amy."

"That's a great idea," Grace said. "She'll love that." Then she handed Ruby an album from the bottom shelf of the coffee table. "Don't forget this one."

"This looks familiar," Ruby said. "It's from a trip to Aruba that we all took five years ago." As Ruby flipped through the pages, she suddenly grew pale.

"Are you okay?" Connie asked.

Ruby pointed to the album on her lap. "Now I know why this album looks familiar. I was looking through it at Tammy's house a few weeks ago. I know that it belongs to Tammy, because I recognize her handwriting in the photo descriptions beneath the pictures."

"So, what's the big deal?" Grace asked. "Tammy might have made one for Sally, too."

"I don't think so. Tammy mentioned that Sally had always admired it, and she was thinking of giving it to her. She said looking through the album reminded her of some of the good times we all had together, and she was considering reaching out to Sally. With everything that happened, I forgot all about it."

Tears filled Ruby's eyes as she realized what this meant. "Tammy must have been here at some point in the last couple of weeks. Why would she lie and tell us she hadn't seen Sally in months?"

Grace sighed. "I guess you'll have to ask her."

Ruby's mood seemed low after discovering the photo album, so Connie and Grace tried to distract her by getting back to work.

"Let's try to make a little headway in the office before we call it a night," Grace suggested.

They boxed up Sally's office supplies and printer to donate. Then they began loading Sally's files into another box so Ruby could sort through them at home.

Connie was about to seal the box when she noticed a file folder entitled 'Community Food Bank.' She pulled out several documents and examined them. They looked like budget printouts from the last few years.

"I wonder if this is connected to what Sally found on Kyle's computer," Ruby said.

Connie examined the budgets more closely. "According to this, there has been a steady decline in donations over the past year. But that doesn't make any sense. Pamela told me that donations were *up* because of Sally's fundraising dinners. Sally must have seen this that day she was working in Kyle's office and questioned him. That would explain the tension between them and why Kyle never asked for her help again."

"This certainly moves Kyle to the top of the suspect list," Ruby said.

"Agreed. You need to show this to the police, Ruby," Connie said.

"Happily," Ruby said. "Maybe this will take some pressure off Amy."

Chapter 10

AS THE WOMEN were walking back to their cars, they noticed one of Sally's neighbors watching from a swing on her porch. The women waved and went over to say hello.

"You must be Sally's family. My name is Cathy. Sally and I had been neighbors since I moved into the neighborhood a few years ago."

"Nice to meet you," Ruby said. "I'm Ruby, Sally's sister-in-law, and these are my friends Connie and Grace."

"Sally was a lovely neighbor. I was shocked to hear what happened." Cathy shivered. "And to think, I was inside my house the entire time."

"It must have been awful when you learned what happened. Did you hear anything unusual coming from Sally's house?" Connie asked.

"Not a thing. The first indication I had that something was wrong was when I heard the police sirens turning onto our street. At least it was the first indication that day."

"What do you mean?" Connie asked. "Did you notice something suspicious on another day?"

"Only once. There was a woman who came to visit Sally a few days before she was killed. They were having a heated discussion right there on Sally's front stairs. I couldn't hear everything they said, but I think they were fighting about a guy named Tim."

"Maybe it was Patsy," Ruby said. "But even if you described her, we don't know what she looks like."

Connie thought for a moment, then held up her index finger. "Just give me two minutes." Using her smartphone Connie went into one of Ruby's social media accounts and from there, found Sally's profile. Then from Sally's page she found Tim, and from there, searched for Patsy. She didn't need the last name, since Tim only had one connection named Patsy. She clicked on it, and a photo of a woman in her mid-fifties, with brown curls popped up. Finally, she showed Cathy Patsy's profile picture.

"Is this the woman?"

"Yup, that's her," Cathy said.

"Can we ask you one more question?" Connie asked.

"Fire away," Cathy said.

"How was Sally's relationship with her other next-door neighbors?" Connie gestured toward Gloria and Don's house.

"It wasn't great," Cathy said. "Sally was convinced that Gloria and Don waited until she went away to build their garage. It was a lawsuit waiting to happen. Gloria and Don were furious when Sally confronted them. I could hear them arguing all the way at my house."

"Furious enough to kill her?" Ruby asked.

"I wouldn't have thought so, but I, for one, lock my doors every night now. No matter who killed Sally, one thing is certain: There is a killer on the loose in Sapphire Beach."

When Connie left Sally's, she stopped at *Just Jewelry* to see how Abby was faring. Since she had everything under control, Connie opted to head home for a relaxing Friday evening in her condo.

After taking Ginger for a long walk and pulling together a dinner from leftovers, Connie sat on the couch with Ginger by her feet to catch up on some reading.

About 8:30 a text came from Zach. *I just stopped by the store, and Abby told me you had left for the night. I have some news.*

Connie replied, *I'm at home if you want to stop by.*

His reply came instantly. *Be right over.*

Within ten minutes, Zach was sitting across from Connie enjoying a cold beer. Judging from his cheerful expression and the enthusiasm in his voice, whatever he wanted to tell her was good news.

"The suspense is killing me," Connie said. "What's your news?"

"I bought a house," he said. "Elyse just called a couple of hours ago to let me know that the sellers signed the Purchase and Sale Agreement."

"That is fantastic," Connie said. "Congratulations!"

"I didn't want to tell you until I was sure the deal wasn't going to fall through. It's one of those bungalows, a few streets over from where Stephanie lives."

"Wow, that's exactly what you were hoping for," Connie said. "I'm so happy for you."

"It's even better than what I was hoping for. It's located next to a canal. It has a beautiful little lanai, and many of the rooms have canal views. It comes with a boat lift and everything."

Connie had a rough idea of what Zach's budget was and also how much those canal homes cost. She tried hide her confusion, but Zach must have seen it on her face, because he started laughing.

"I know what you're thinking. You're wondering if I robbed a bank."

Connie nearly choked on her wine. "I trust you didn't break the law, but canal houses are expensive. Did you win the lottery and forget to tell me?"

"I feel like I did, but no. I bought a fixer upper - and by fixer upper, I mean a complete gut job. It's in horrible shape and it has three small bedrooms and one bathroom, so not as big as some of the other canal homes. But it's all mine. Or at least it will be soon. If all goes well, it will be mine on February 21."

Zach went on about all the plans he had for his new home. "The bedrooms are small, but they will work when my family visits. I can't wait to get my hands on it."

"I'm so happy. By the time you finish it will be exactly what you wanted."

"I owe Elyse big. She cut her commission in half so that I could afford it. I'll obviously have to hire out some of the work, but I'll do what I can myself. During high school and college, I worked summers and vacations with my uncle in construction, so I know how to do some things. That will help save on labor."

"That is such great news, Zach. I can't wait to see it."

The smile never left Zach's face the whole time he talked about the house. Connie couldn't ever remember seeing Zach this talkative.

"It will take most of my savings to fix it up, but Elyse assures me it will be a strong investment. I'll have instant equity if I do it right. That reminds me, I'd love for you to help me choose the finishes. I'll need a new bathroom and kitchen, and I'll have to choose paint color and flooring, not to mention light fixtures. There are so many options to choose from that I'm not sure where to start, and I know your family is in the design business." Connie's mother and sister were professional home stagers and, if Connie did say so herself, she had absorbed a good amount of their expertise over the years.

"I would love to help. We should start looking soon so that once you pass papers and are ready to begin, everything will be chosen, and you can just place the order. That way there will be no delays on construction."

"How about next Sunday night? I know it's easier for you to break away on a Sunday night than a Saturday. We could have dinner first, then shop afterwards."

"Sounds perfect," Connie said.

"And I'll tell Elyse that I'd like to get into the house one more time so I can do some measuring, as well. That way I can hit the ground running when I pass papers. Hopefully, things will slow down at work. It will be hard to renovate a house while working extra hours at the same time."

"You have a full plate right now," Connie said. "How is the investigation into Sally's murder going? Ruby is devastated that her newly discovered niece inadvertently became involved." She decided not to mention anything about Tammy just yet.

"Since I'm in the middle of a house hunt, Josh is taking the lead on that investigation. But I know Ruby stopped by to show us some financial paperwork that she found when you were with her cleaning out Sally's house. How is it that you are somehow connected to every murder that takes place in Sapphire Beach?" Zach asked playfully.

"I wish I knew," Connie said.

When Zach finished his beer, he left to pull together some paperwork for his bank. He wanted to do everything possible to keep the process rolling smoothly so he could get into the house and begin renovations.

Connie walked him to the door, and he gave her a gentle kiss before leaving. As Zach left, Connie noticed she was wearing a smile almost as broad as Zach's. His enthusiasm was contagious.

Chapter 11

ON SATURDAY MORNING, inspired by the unseasonably warm temperature, Connie woke up early to go for a quick paddle along the coastline. Her kayaking expedition last Sunday had her thinking about getting back out onto the water all week, so she decided to seize the day. Or at least the morning. She took her paddleboard out of her storage closet in the garage, loaded it onto the carrier, and wheeled it to the beach. After a thirty minute paddle, she sat on her board, allowing the morning sun to shine on her face and the gentle waves to push her into shore. Then she headed upstairs for a shower.

On her way to *Just Jewelry,* Connie dropped off the trash bags filled with Sally's clothing at the donation center of her church's thrift shop and arrived just in time to open the store with Grace at 9:00. Connie was glad that she had taken some time to herself, because she barely had a chance to take a break all day.

The following week was uneventful. As usual, Connie spent every day at the store, taking advantage of the mornings when Grace was working to get back into a regular workout routine, either outdoors or in the gym at Palm Paradise. When Grace or Abby were in the store, Connie managed to find a few chunks of time to take stock of her inventory and place another order with her Fair Trade artisans. Connie still had plenty of pieces that she created in the storage room, so she didn't have to worry about replenishing her stock quite yet, but she ordered some beads and other supplies to have on hand for when she was able to devote some time to jewelry-making.

Around dinnertime on Friday, just as things started to slow down, Connie's phone pinged. It was a group text from Ruby to Connie and Grace. *Amy was in a car accident and is at the Gulf Coast Medical Center in Fort Myers. I think someone might have tried to hurt her.*

Next came a message from Grace. *I'm running some errands in the area. I'll be right there.*

Since Abby had things under control in the shop, Connie decided to drop Ginger off at home and head over for moral support.

Within a half hour, all three women were at Amy's bedside in the emergency room. Amy didn't appear to have any serious injuries, but she was shaken up.

"Tell us what happened," Connie said.

"It was dark, and I was heading home after running some errands when I noticed a car in my rearview mirror that seemed to be following me. At first, I told myself I was letting my imagination get the best of me. I made a few turns to try to lose the car, but every time I turned, it stayed on my tail. I decided it would be safer to go back toward a main road, but the driver got more aggressive. He or she tapped my rear bumper with the front of their car, and that's when I really started to panic. The car pulled up beside me and pushed me off the road and into a tree. Then it sped off. My head was throbbing, so I called 911 right away, but he was long gone."

"Did you see the driver?" Connie asked.

"No, it was too dark. I couldn't even tell if it was a man or a woman. He or she wore a black hoodie with the hood pulled up. By the time the car had pulled up alongside me, I was too scared to notice anything, except that the car was black."

While they were talking, Amy's doctor came in and said they were going to do a scan to be sure there was no internal bleeding, and if not, Amy would be released later that night.

A few minutes later, a woman with straight brown hair and worried eyes ran into the hospital room and threw her arms around Amy. "I got here as soon as I could. Are you okay, honey?"

"I'm okay, Mom, just a little shaken up."

In her concern for her daughter, the woman hadn't noticed Connie, Grace, and Ruby.

Ruby extended her hand. "You must be Jody. I'm Ruby Boyd. I'm Kevin's sister."

The woman's expression grew pensive. "Hi Ruby, it's nice to meet you."

"I just want you to know how happy I am that Amy has come into my life. It has been a real honor getting to know her. She reminds me so much of Kevin."

The woman frowned. "That is very kind of you, so it makes what I have to say even harder, but I'd appreciate it if you'd keep your distance from Amy for now. Don't get me wrong, I'm happy that Amy had to the chance to connect with you, and I am grateful for the acceptance that you have shown her, but Amy's contact with your family has become too dangerous. First, Kevin's widow is murdered, and my daughter is a suspect. Then, she is run off the road and almost killed. I'm sure you can understand my concern."

"Mom, that's not fair," Amy said. "None of that is Ruby's fault."

Ruby looked at Amy, fighting back tears. "Your mother's right, Amy. She has good reason to be concerned for your safety. As much as I want to continue our relationship and introduce you to the rest of the family, this is getting too dangerous. We should honor your mother's wishes."

Jody breathed a sigh of relief. "Thank you for understanding."

"I only ask that Amy send me a quick text when she is released from the hospital, so I know she is okay," Ruby said.

"Of course," Jody said.

"Mom, can I have a few minutes to say goodbye to my friends?"

Jody's expression softened. "Fair enough. I'll go get a coffee."

Amy waited for Jody to leave, then said, "Connie, I know that you've helped the police solve murder cases in the past. Please, promise me you'll do everything you can to put the real killer behind bars. It's the only way I'll ever get to meet the rest of my father's family. I don't have the heart to go against my mother's wishes, but if you find the killer, she'll have no reason to object to my meeting my father's family."

Connie couldn't refuse Amy's request. "I promise I'll do my best."

"Thank you," Amy said. "Then I'll say, 'See you soon,' instead of 'Goodbye.'"

Ruby hugged Amy, "Absolutely. I'll see you soon."

Ruby's shoulders drooped low as the women left Amy's hospital room. Ruby looked like a scared little girl who was trying to put on a brave face. Grace looped her arm through Ruby's to support her friend as they walked to the elevator.

The three women had arrived at the hospital in separate cars, and Connie and Grace didn't want to leave Ruby alone yet, so when they arrived in the hospital lobby, they led Ruby to a couch in front of a large picture window.

"I'm so sorry," Grace said, as they settled onto the sofa. "I know this is not how you wanted things to turn out with Amy."

Tears filled Ruby's eyes, and Connie fished a tissue from her pocketbook.

"It feels like I'm losing Kevin all over again," she said, dabbing her eyes. Her expression grew distant, as if she were thinking of another place and time. "Kevin was my rock. I don't talk about this very often, but just before I moved to Sapphire Beach, I was involved with a man named Danny. I thought the sun rose and set on him. We were crazy about each other and planning to be married. After a while, Danny began to spend time with people I wasn't comfortable with, and eventually he started using drugs. I was heartbroken, but I somehow believed I could fix him. One night, I caught him stealing cash from my wallet and I confronted him. Instead of being sorry, he became violent. To make a long story short, finally Danny left, and I called Kevin. He came straight over to find me crying with a black eye. I was terrified. I had tried to break up with Danny, but he threatened me."

Ruby leaned back and closed her eyes. "I don't know what Kevin said to Danny, but he never bothered me again. About six months later, we lost our parents. I was still in a funk over Danny, so Kevin convinced Tammy and Glen to sell me their share of our parents' home in Sapphire Beach. He believed in me so much that he gave me a loan to buy them out and open the souvenir shop. When Kevin died, it was more than losing a big brother. He was my protector and my best friend. Meeting Amy was like having a piece of Kevin back in my life. I was going to be the best aunt I could be. And Amy and her fiancé want to have children right away, so I was going to be a great-aunt, too. What am I going to do?" Ruby took Connie's hands in hers. "Promise me you'll find Sally's killer so that I can have Amy back in my life and justice for my brother's widow."

Connie's heart broke for Ruby. How could she say no?

For the second time that evening, she found herself promising she would do everything she could to find Sally's killer.

Chapter 12

IT WAS NEARLY 9:00 by the time Connie and Grace left Ruby, so there was no point going back to *Just Jewelry*. Abby would be closing up shop before she could get there. Instead, she headed home.

Connie and Grace pulled into the underground parking garage at Palm Paradise at the same time, so as they were riding the elevator to the seventh floor, Connie invited Grace over for a cup of herbal tea.

"Poor Ruby," Grace said, as Connie brought two steaming mugs into the living room.

"I know. My heart is breaking for her," Connie said. "We need to figure out who killed Sally so Ruby can have Amy back in her life."

"Why do you suppose whoever killed Sally decided to run Amy off the road?" Grace asked. "Why would the killer want to hurt Amy?"

"Since Amy was the prime suspect, it doesn't make sense that the killer would want to eliminate her," Connie said. "In my opinion, the killer was trying to send us a message. If his or her goal was to kill Amy, she would be in much worse shape right now. I think it was a scare tactic to stop us from asking any more questions."

"Makes sense," Grace said. "If that's true, I suppose the silver lining in Amy's accident is that we've made the killer nervous. That means we're on the right track."

"That's a good point," Connie said. "And the other positive outcome from Amy's accident is that the police will have to remove Amy from their list of suspects," Connie said.

"That should give Ruby some consolation. Who is on the top of your list now?" Grace asked. "Who do you think we scared enough to make a desperate move?"

Connie thought about the past couple of weeks, and the people they had talked with and observed.

"There are a few people who come to mind. Now that we know that Sally likely suspected Kyle of embezzling money, Kyle is a strong suspect."

"And don't forget about his son, Jack," Grace said.

"Jack's behavior was definitely odd when Ruby and I were at the food bank. It's possible that Jack could have killed Sally to protect his father and driven Amy off the road to scare us away."

"That would be a shame," Grace said. "I'd hate to see negative publicity fall upon Community Food Bank because of one bad apple. So many people rely on them when times get tough."

Connie ran a hand through her dark brown hair. "Then there's Patsy, Tim's jealous girlfriend. Sally's neighbor, Cathy, saw her at Sally's house shortly before Sally was murdered. She could have seen Sally as a threat to her happiness and returned to kill her."

"Don't forget Gloria," Grace said. "I still can't believe she took Sally's platter."

"And built the garage while Sally was away," Connie said.

"What a piece of work. And don't forget her husband, Don. He is the one who built the garage," Grace said.

Connie and Grace sipped their tea in silence.

"I know neither of us wants to talk about the elephant in the room, but we can't rule Tammy out. She was very angry at Sally for making Kevin work so hard, and Ruby and Tammy both believe that contributed to his early death."

Grace nodded reluctantly. "I don't like that we found Tammy's photo album at Sally's. Ruby said she saw the same album at Tammy's house only a couple of weeks before. That means that Tammy lied to us about seeing Sally recently."

"I sure hope for Ruby's sake that Tammy didn't do it," Connie said. "But we have to keep her on the list."

"Although, in Tammy's defense, if she did pay a visit to Sally to make peace by bringing her the photo album, I think it's unlikely she would have killed Sally," Grace said.

"Let's hope you're right. But don't forget, it was an emotionally volatile situation. Tammy could have gone to Sally's with good intentions, but perhaps

Sally did or said something to bring Tammy's anger to the surface, and she killed her. We know it was a crime of passion, because the killer used a nearby lamp as the murder weapon. It clearly wasn't premeditated."

Grace let out a deep breath and nodded. "I guess you're right. So, what's your plan, now that you've officially promised both Amy and Ruby you would help?"

"I'd like to talk to everyone again in light of what happened to Amy. Some of the people on our suspect list might have alibis for last night. With a little luck, we can rule some of them out."

"That sounds like a good plan. Please let me know what I can do to help. I'd do anything for Ruby," Grace said.

"Will do." Connie took a long sip of tea and tried to gather her courage. "On a completely different note, I've been meaning to talk to you about something."

Grace placed her empty mug on the coffee table. "Sounds serious."

"Well, kind of. As you know, I had a wonderful morning on Sunday, kayaking around the Matlacha Pass Aquatic Preserve, thanks to you."

"You're welcome honey, but you already thanked me for that."

"I am grateful, but that's not what I wanted to tell you." Connie took a deep breath. She hoped she wasn't crossing any boundaries. "I had a chance to talk to Brenda while I was kayaking. She was also on the trip."

Grace crossed her arms and opened her mouth to say something, but Connie cut her off.

"I know she hurt you by not staying in Sapphire Beach when Aunt Concetta got sick," Connie said. "But did you know that she had recently lost her sister to colon cancer and couldn't bear to go through that again?"

"I wasn't aware." Grace shook her head. "But that's not an excuse. It wasn't about Brenda; it was about Concetta."

"I know how you feel, but I can also understand her feelings. She had just watched her sister go through the same battle. She just didn't have the strength to go through it again. But she does love you, and she loved Concetta. I know she regrets her decision."

"She told you that?"

Connie nodded.

"You're telling me to just *forgive* her? To forget how she disappeared when we needed her the most?"

Connie put her hand on Grace's. "I'm asking you to try. I hate seeing you carry that bitterness. You are neighbors after all, and she was a good friend."

Grace gazed out the glass slider and into the darkness. When she looked back at Connie, her expression had softened. "To tell you the truth. I've been thinking about Brenda a lot lately. If Ruby can forgive Sally for what she did to her brother, I guess I can try, too. I'll think about it."

Connie hugged Grace. "Thank you. That's all I ask. I'll be praying that God gives you the strength."

"Thanks honey, I'll need it."

The following morning, Ruby came by *Just Jewelry* to give Connie and Grace an update on Amy.

"I received a text late last night from Amy saying that her x-rays and scans came back clear and that she was home resting. She is going to stay at her mother's house until the killer is caught, but the doctor told her that she should be back to normal after a few days' rest."

Grace put her arm around Ruby's shoulder. "That's great news. At least you know she'll be safe."

"Now, if we could only catch the killer, we could put this whole nightmare behind us."

"It's good to see you looking on the positive side," Grace said.

"That's because there are two very positive things that came out of Amy's accident. The first is that when Amy texted me last night, she said the police were no longer treating her as a suspect. And the second is that Tammy has an alibi for last night. She and Ray were out to dinner with a few other couples during the time Amy was run off the road. So, Tammy is off the suspect list as well."

"That's wonderful news," Grace said.

"I just hope that once we find the killer, Jody will have no reason to keep Amy away from us."

Chapter 13

BEFORE CONNIE KNEW IT, Sunday afternoon had arrived. As soon as Abby came for her evening shift, Connie scooted out to meet Zach to help him choose finishes for his soon-to-be new home. She dropped off her silver Jetta at Palm Paradise, and Zach picked her up outside the lobby.

"I'm looking forward to this," Connie said, hopping into the passenger side of his gray Jeep. "It's always fun spending someone else's money."

Since Connie's mother and sister owned a home staging company, normally, they were the experts in the family when it came to all things home décor. But Connie had to admit, she enjoyed being the one with the most design expertise for a change.

They stopped for a quick burger, then headed to a big box store to get some ideas. After getting Zach's thoughts on a variety of designs, Connie dubbed his style as modern-beachy. Once Connie had a better sense of his taste, she made some suggestions for the kitchen. Since the space was small, she suggested a lighter kitchen, so Zach decided on white shaker cabinets to brighten it up, and a seafoam blue island with matching backsplash.

Next, they went to the flooring department. Because of the humid, subtropical climate in Sapphire Beach, tile was the most practical choice of materials. Plus, they would be easy to keep clean. The sheer number of flooring choices was overwhelming, but Zach finally decided on porcelain tile designed to look like hardwood floors, which would contrast nicely with the white cabinets.

Choosing the paint color was surprisingly easy. Zach already knew he wanted the same warm gray that Connie had in her store. She had learned from her mother and sister that gray walls made for the perfect neutral backdrop for art and photos.

For the countertops, they headed to a granite and marble warehouse. Zach would need a contractor before he could place an order, but they looked around, anyway, to get some ideas. Since they were going for a beachy feel, Connie suggested choosing honed granite, rather than glossy, for a more natural look. They would have to return when Zach was further along in the process, but after viewing a variety of samples, Zach was leaning toward a beige, white, and gray granite with a lot of movement, which made Connie think of the rocky New England beaches.

Connie wrote down all of Zach's top choices. The only room they hadn't worked on was the bathroom, but they decided to save it for another day. Just when Connie thought she couldn't look at another flooring, paint, or backsplash sample, Zach dropped Connie off at Palm Paradise.

"Don't forget about our Valentine's Day date on Friday," he said as he walked her to the elevator. He had informed her earlier that he had a surprise in store.

"Are you going to give me any hints as to where we are going?" she asked.

He kissed her and said with a playful smile. "Not a chance."

By the time Zach left, it was getting late, so after taking Ginger for a walk, Connie curled up on her recliner with a book and relaxed for the rest of the night.

Throughout the day on Monday, a consistent stream of customers trickled in and out of the shop. Before Grace left for the day, Connie went out to take Ginger for a walk and pick up a sandwich for lunch. As she was strolling down the street, Ruby came up behind her.

"Do you mind if I join you?" Ruby asked.

"I'd love the company. How are you holding up?"

"I'm ready for this whole ordeal to be over. I just want to know who killed my sister-in-law so that she can rest in peace and Amy can meet the rest of the family."

Connie stopped suddenly, startling poor Ginger. "Ruby, you're off the crutches!"

Ruby laughed. "I was wondering how long it would take you to notice."

"I was about to get a sandwich," Connie said. "Have you eaten yet?"

"Not yet. How about if after our sandwiches we get an ice cream to celebrate my recovery?" Ruby said.

"You don't have to twist my arm."

They went to the nearest sandwich shop and took their lunch to a bench by the beach. Although the temperature was only in the high 60s, the sun was strong in the cloudless sky and the beach was teeming with sunbathers and children playing in the water. Although it was now early February, the weather reminded Connie of a June day in Boston.

Connie tried to get Ruby's mind off the investigation by chatting about their businesses and life in Sapphire Beach. When they finished their sandwiches, they went into Friendly Scoops, where they chatted with the owner, Emily, then took their ice creams to an outside table to enjoy the fresh air. As they were people watching and finishing their cones, Connie's eyes were drawn to a couple walking towards the pier.

Ruby followed Connie's gaze to the couple, strolling along and holding hands. "Is that who I think it is?"

"That looks like Tim, and I think I recognize Patsy from her profile picture. Let's try to talk to them. Maybe we can find out why Patsy visited Sally just before she was killed."

Connie stood up just as they passed in front of their table and called out Tim's name.

"Connie, Ruby, how nice to see you," Tim said as he and Patsy came over to their table. Given all the probing questions Connie had asked Tim the last time they talked, she was relieved that he didn't run in the opposite direction.

After exchanging small talk for a couple of minutes, it was Tim who moved the conversation to the investigation. "I know you ladies were taking it upon yourselves to try to clear your niece's name," Tim said to Ruby.

"And we were so sorry to hear about what happened to Sally," Patsy added.

Connie studied Patsy, trying to decide if she seemed sincere.

"But just in case you are still investigating, please know we talked with the police earlier today. They told us about what happened to Amy and questioned Patsy on her whereabouts at the time of her accident.

There is no way that Patsy could have caused Amy's accident. Ever since she was in a car accident six months ago, Patsy has been afraid to get behind the wheel. She never replaced her car and takes an Uber whenever she goes out alone."

"I am working on getting over my fear of driving, but for now, I spend the money I would be paying toward a car payment and insurance on rideshare apps when I go out alone."

"She practices her driving," Tim said, "but only on streets with little traffic. There is no way she could have pushed Amy's car off the road."

It sounded like a solid alibi, as long as they were telling the truth.

"We were told that you paid Sally a visit the week before she died," Connie said. "Is that true?"

"Yes, it's true. I only recently told Tim, so he didn't know that when you last talked. I went to Sally's house to ask what her intentions were with Tim. She assured me that she wasn't looking for a relationship with anyone and wished me well. I didn't believe her, which led to a heated discussion, then I left. But you must believe me, even if she did want to be with Tim, I never would have hurt her."

"Thank you for letting us know," Ruby said. "We know you are not obligated to talk to us."

"It's the least we can do for Sally's family after such a tragedy," Tim said. "I don't think I properly expressed my condolences the last time we talked. I was a bit on the defensive when we spoke, since it seemed like you were accusing Patsy of murder. But in hindsight, I understand that you were just exploring all avenues. I'm sure I would be asking a lot of questions, too, if one of my family members was murdered."

"Thank you for understanding," Ruby said. "And thank you for being a good friend to Sally."

After their conversation with Tim and Patsy, Connie and Ruby took the long way back to their stores, in order to give Ginger a little more exercise before being cooped up in the shop for the rest of the day.

"What do you think of Patsy's alibi?" Ruby asked.

"I tend to think she's telling the truth. If she's afraid to drive, I doubt she could be aggressive enough behind the wheel to force Amy off the road. It would be quite the elaborate scheme if she were faking her fear of driving. I'm moving her to the bottom of my list, but I'm not removing her completely," Connie said. "First, I want to verify her story with Cathy. If Cathy saw her leaving Sally's, she would know whether she was driving that day, or whether she took an Uber."

Chapter 14

SINCE GRACE WAS WORKING in the store on Monday morning, Connie planned to meet Ruby at Sally's to continue sorting through Sally's personal belongings. The plan was for Connie to help Ruby in the morning, then return to *Just Jewelry* to take over for Grace, who would help Ruby in the afternoon. They hoped that after a full day's work, the job would be complete.

Grace was afraid that Ruby was doing too much too soon, so to humor her, Ruby promised to keep her crutches close by in case she got tired and needed them.

Connie and Ruby picked up right where they left off, sorting Sally's possessions into piles designated as items to keep, donate, or throw away. They finished with the guest bedrooms, then moved to the kitchen.

"Are you sure you want to keep all these items?" Connie asked, referring to a pile of kitchenware. "I don't think you can fit them in your house, and I'm sure Tammy's and Glen's homes are already furnished."

"I have a few ideas for them," Ruby said. "I can always donate them later if they don't find a home."

A couple of hours into their work, there was a loud knock at the front door.

"I'll get it," Ruby said.

Connie watched over the kitchen island as Ruby opened the door. It was Don, holding the lavender serving dish that they had brought over the last time they were there. At least Connie thought it was. She couldn't be certain, since the dish was filled with brownies.

"Please come in," Ruby said. "I'm sorry, but I can't even offer you a cup of coffee. We just put the coffee maker into one of these boxes, and I'm not sure which one."

Connie put the dishes she was packing back down on the counter and joined Ruby and Don. They had stepped into the foyer, but Don didn't appear to want to go any further.

"I can't stay long," Don said, handing Ruby the platter filled with thick, dark brownies. "I just wanted to return your platter. I think my wife was mistaken when she took it. It resembles a dish that we have, but after examining it more closely, she realized that it's not ours. To make up for the confusion, Gloria baked you a batch of her famous double fudge brownies. I hope you can accept our apology."

"Thank you," Ruby said, graciously accepting the dish. "That was very kind of her. And unnecessary. These things happen."

Connie suspected Don and Gloria were suddenly being neighborly in hopes that Ruby would forget about the garage.

"I know we got off to a bad start, but my wife's bark is bigger than her bite. It's true that she wasn't the biggest fan of Sally, especially after she threatened us with a lawsuit over the garage, but I hope you don't think that my wife could be involved in Sally's murder. She even felt guilty about taking the serving dish and started baking brownies when she saw you arrive here."

Connie didn't envy Elyse's job of having to get her hands on a permit that Connie was pretty sure didn't exist.

"I heard there was some tension over the garage," Ruby said.

"I guess you could say that, but you must understand, our garage is completely on our property. It doesn't even touch Sally's and Kevin's yard. Maybe technically we were supposed to leave more space between our garage and their yard, but it was an honest mistake and it wasn't hurting anyone. Sally could have just let it go, instead of insisting that we waste thousands of dollars tearing down a perfectly good garage, but, no, she was out there as soon as she returned from her trip with her measuring tape and notebook. Sally may have had money to spare, but some of us live on a budget."

"I can understand your frustration," Connie said. "But Sally and Gloria were seen fighting about it on a number of occasions in the months before Sally was killed."

Connie hoped she didn't get Don so mad that he'd take the brownies back. They looked good.

But he didn't. Instead, he let out a deep sigh. "I can't deny that my wife and Sally fought, but I can assure you, Gloria wouldn't hurt her worst enemy. She called me at work horrified when the police came, and she was devastated to learn what had happened to Sally."

"May I ask you another question?" Connie asked.

"Sure, go ahead."

"Where were you and your wife on Friday afternoon about 4:00?"

"Both Gloria and I were at friend's house playing bocce," Don said, without even having to think about it. "Their gated community has a bocce court, and a bunch of us get together every Friday for our weekly tournament. Why do you ask?"

"My niece was in a car accident, and we believe the same person who killed Sally also ran Amy's car off the road to scare us away from investigating," Ruby said.

Don seemed genuinely surprised to learn of Amy's accident. "Well, there are at least ten people who can vouch for us. Now will you believe me that neither me nor my wife had anything to do with Sally's death?"

"We appreciate the information," Connie said. "And thanks again for bringing the dish back."

"I don't want to keep you," Don said. "I see that you have a lot of work to do. If you need a hand carrying any boxes to your car, let me know. I'm happy to help."

"Thank you," Ruby said. "I might just take you up on that if we don't finish up today."

Connie and Ruby returned to work for another hour before Connie had to get back to the store to relieve Grace. Before she left, Connie suggested they pay a quick visit to Cathy in order to verify Patsy's story about not driving.

Fortunately, Cathy was sitting on the front porch once again, enjoying the early afternoon sun and sipping a beverage.

Connie waved, and she and Ruby walked over to Cathy's porch.

Cathy invited them to join her on the hunter green wicker chairs. "Let me get you a glass of lemonade," she said. But before they could answer, she disappeared into the house, returning a couple of minutes later carrying a pitcher and two pink plastic glasses filled with ice.

Connie took the glasses and placed them on the table while Cathy poured the drinks. "This is my special homemade lemonade, made from fresh lemon juice and raw honey."

"This is amazing," Ruby said, after taking a sip. "It's the perfect combination of sweet and tart."

Cathy smiled. "It's my favorite thing to drink while watching the day go by from my porch." Her smile faded. "Every so often Sally and I would have a glass together. I sure hope the police can bring her killer to justice."

"So do we," Ruby said.

Cathy pointed her index finger toward Ruby. "Now, you promise me when you sell this house, that you'll find me some pleasant neighbors."

"I will pass your request along to Elyse," Ruby said. "We will do our best."

"Speaking of Sally's killer," Connie said, "while we're here, we wanted to double check on something. You mentioned the last time we saw you that a woman, whom we determined was Patsy, came to visit Sally a few days before she passed away. Do you remember if Patsy drove herself or if someone gave her a ride?"

"She definitely got a ride," Cathy said. "I remember, because she was standing at the end of the driveway waiting for about five minutes, after storming out of Sally's house and before she was picked up."

Connie thanked her for the information, and after finishing her lemonade, left Ruby and Cathy on the porch so she could get back to *Just Jewelry*.

When she turned on her car, Connie checked the time. She still had forty-five minutes before she needed to be back to the shop, so Connie decided to make a quick stop at Community Food Bank. She had loaded a couple of boxes of office supplies from Sally's house into her trunk, so she thought she'd see if Pamela could use them at the food bank.

When Connie arrived, Pamela was instructing a group of volunteers, so Connie waited until she was finished before approaching.

"Connie," Pamela said when she finally noticed her, "what a surprise. What brings you by the food bank today?"

"I came by to make a donation on Sally's behalf. Over the past couple of weeks, Ruby, Grace, and I have been cleaning out Sally's house, and we thought you might be able to put her office supplies to good use," Connie said. "I have a couple of boxes full of paper, envelopes, and other general office items in my car. I know when I used to work for a nonprofit, any office supplies that were donated meant more money in our budget to go toward our mission."

Pamela's eyes grew wide. "How kind of you to think of us. We can always use things like that. Let me get Jack to carry the boxes from your car."

Connie was about to protest and tell Pamela that she could carry in the boxes herself, but it was too late. The next thing she knew, she was showing Jack to her car.

As they walked in silence, Jack never once made eye contact with her.

"Thanks for your help, Jack," Connie finally said, while he carried the boxes across the parking lot and into the building.

"Thank you for the donation," he said. "Now, I trust that you have no reason left to return to the food bank."

Connie looked at him, startled, but Jack was looking straight ahead.

"I'm too busy to volunteer at the moment, but you never know what reason I might have for stopping by in the future."

Although Jack wasn't looking at Connie, she could feel the anger rising from him like steam. If he were dangerous, the last thing she wanted to do was instigate him, but she certainly wasn't going to be bullied by him, either.

Suddenly, Jack stopped and put the boxes down abruptly in front of a white Kia. Connie thought he was about to tell her off, when he surprised her by fishing a key from his pocket and opening the car door. He leaned into the car, grabbed a folder, and picked up the boxes again.

"Just needed to get something out of my car," he said.

They finally made it to Pamela's office. Jack placed the boxes on the floor near Pamela's storage cabinet, glared at Connie momentarily, and left.

"I don't know what's gotten into that young man," Pamela said. "He barely says a word these days."

"Maybe he's just moody," Connie suggested.

Pamela appeared to be considering that explanation. "He can be moody. Come to think of it, his father has been making him work extra shifts at the food bank," Pamela said. "Maybe he'd just rather be with his friends."

"That must be it," Connie said. As she was preparing to leave, Connie suddenly realized something. Jack's car was white, not black, like the car that drove Amy off the road. That meant Jack couldn't be the killer. But if he wasn't, why was he so visibly angry at Connie?

Pamela chuckled. "You have the strangest expression on your face. What are you thinking about?"

"I suppose I can tell you now," Connie said. She explained to Pamela about Jack's strange behavior, Amy being driven off the road by a black car and how she just learned that Jack's care was white.

"Jack's car is his baby," Pamela said. "He flipped burgers for years to buy that car. There's no way he'd intentionally hit another car with it. And in case you're wondering, Kyle's car is silver."

"Thanks for letting me know," Connie said. "And yes, I was wondering."

Chapter 15

AFTER LEAVING the food bank, Connie stopped by her house to pick up Ginger and make a quick sandwich, then headed to *Just Jewelry* so that Grace could get to Sally's.

"Sorry I'm late," Connie said, glancing at the time on her phone. "I made a couple of stops on the way." Connie went on to tell Grace about Ruby and her conversations with Don and Cathy, as well as what she learned at the food bank from Pamela, particularly that neither Kyle nor Jack drove a black car.

"You've had a busy morning," Grace said. "No wonder you're running late. I'll take Ginger for a walk before I meet Ruby at Sally's."

"Thanks," Connie said. "You're a lifesaver. I don't think you and Ruby will be able to finish clearing out the Sally's house today. There are still a few more rooms to go through, including the kitchen."

"I'm afraid Ruby is going to reinjure her ankle if she keeps going at this pace," Grace said. "Does she have her crutches with her?"

Connie laughed. "Yes, she kept her promise and has them by her side just in case."

Connie worked alone in *Just Jewelry* for the rest of Monday and Tuesday. The consistent influx of customers didn't give her much time to think about anything except work.

About 3:00 on Tuesday, Connie's phone pinged with a text message from Elyse to Connie and Stephanie, who was Grace's daughter and Connie's friend. In between customers, Connie read the message. *I know it's late notice, but can you ladies meet for drinks tonight? I miss you both. It's been way too long since we've had a girls' night.*

Stephanie had already replied. *I'm in.*

It works for me if we can meet after 9:00. I'm working alone tonight. Drinks and appetizers at 9:30

152

tonight at Surfside? Connie replied, hoping the late hour would work for everyone. She hadn't realized how long it had been since she spent any alone time with Elyse and Stephanie. They were together for several holiday gatherings, but that wasn't the same as hanging out alone.

Elyse and Stephanie both replied with a thumbs up. Connie's energy level skyrocketed for the rest of the afternoon, as she looked forward to some long overdue time with her friends. Finally, 9:00 arrived. Connie closed up shop, brought Ginger home, and arrived at Surfside Restaurant just in time.

"I'm so glad you were both able to make it on such late notice," Elyse said. "It's been far too long since we've hung out, just the three of us."

"I couldn't agree more," Stephanie said.

It was a warm evening, so they requested a table outdoors on the deck. Connie leaned back in her chair and inhaled the fresh, salty air, thrilled to be outdoors on a beautiful evening.

They ordered a few appetizers to share and each ordered a frozen drink, which was more like a dessert than a beverage. Then they caught up on one another's lives.

Stephanie had met a guy through a colleague at work, but after a couple of dates, they mutually decided it wasn't going to work. "I didn't mention it to my mother," Stephanie said to Connie. "So, please don't say anything to her about it. I learned a long time ago that I'm better off not telling her the details of my dating life unless I'm ready to introduce her to someone."

Connie laughed. "Cross my heart."

Connie was also pleased to hear that Elyse's daughters, Emma and Victoria, were continuing to forge a strong sisterly bond. Emma was nine years older than Victoria, having been an only child until she was eleven, when her family adopted then two-year-old Victoria. Emma had a difficult time accepting the change Victoria brought into her life, but that was all in the past. According to Elyse, Emma had become a sensitive and caring big sister.

Connie wasn't surprised.

Elyse fought back a playful smirk. "So, do you and Zach have plans for Valentine's Day?"

"We do, but he won't tell me what we're doing."

"Ooh, a mystery date," Stephanie said. "Sounds like fun."

"I might just know a little something about what he has planned," Elyse teased.

"Are you *serious*? You've got to give me a clue," Connie said.

"And deal with the wrath of Zach? No way! All I can tell you is that he has something special planned, and I think you're going to like it."

"Hmmm, mysterious," Connie said. "I'm still confused about why Zach told *you* about our date and not me, but I guess I have to wait until Friday to find out."

"As much as I am dying to know what Zach has planned, we should probably change the subject before Elyse spills too much," Stephanie said.

"That sounds like a wise idea," Elyse said. "I know Josh's murder investigation involves Ruby Boyd's family and that you and Grace have become friends with her. I don't suppose there's any chance that you haven't gotten involved in the case."

"I really didn't want to but…"

Connie was interrupted by Elyse and Stephanie's laughter.

"How many times have we heard that?" Stephanie said. "Even my mother has accepted that you always get involved, and she was dead set against it the first couple of times."

"It's not so much that I *like* being involved," Connie said. "I just want to see justice served, especially this time, for Ruby's sake."

Connie explained how Amy found Ruby through a DNA website and how well they hit it off. She also told them about Kevin and how much Amy reminded Ruby of her deceased brother. "And now," Connie said, "Amy promised her mother she would cut off contact with Ruby, because her mother was concerned for her safety."

"Poor Ruby," Stephanie said. "So, tell us who you've talked to so far."

"Yeah, Josh doesn't tell me anything about his cases," Elyse said. "All I know is that Ruby Boyd's sister-in-law was the victim, and I only know that because Ruby called me about listing it.

Connie told them the whole story, starting with their first meeting with Tammy and ending with her conversations with Don, Cathy, and Pamela the day before.

"It's amazing how many people are discovering relatives through DNA websites," Stephanie said. "I have a patient who discovered a sister she never knew she had."

"Ruby was thrilled to learn about Amy," Connie said. "She was super close to her brother until he unexpectedly passed away of a heart attack four years ago. Meeting Amy was like getting a piece of her brother back."

"Now I understand why you're so motivated to help Ruby," Stephanie said.

"I don't see how I can say no to her, now that Amy's mother doesn't want her in contact with Ruby or her family. I understand that she is worried about her daughter's safety, but poor Ruby is heartbroken. I just don't have the heart refuse her request."

Connie opted not to mention Grace's role in pulling her into the investigation. She didn't want to get Grace in trouble with Stephanie, since it didn't seem like Stephanie realized how involved her mother was.

"So, it sounds like you've come full circle," Elyse said. "All of your original suspects either have an alibi for Sally's death or an alibi for Amy's accident."

"You're right," Connie said with a sigh. "I'm at a loss. I started off with six suspects, but the evidence seems to rule all of them out. Amy said that the car that hit her was black. Kyle's car is silver and Jack's is white. Tammy and Patsy both have alibis for when Amy was hit, and so do Don and Gloria. Gloria was home alone when Sally was killed, but during Amy's accident, Gloria and Don were both with at least ten other people."

"Then it must be someone you haven't thought of yet," Stephanie said. "If none of your suspects are guilty, there must be someone else who had a motive to kill Sally that you don't know about yet."

"Right," Connie said, leaning her forearms on the table. "I'm back at square one." She polished off the last of the nachos and took a sip of her pina colada, then leaned back in her chair.

"Connie," Elyse said. "You just told us that Gloria was alone when Sally was killed, but when we were at Gloria and Don's house, they said they were both at home together."

Connie thought for a moment. "Elyse, you're a genius."

"Thank you," Elyse said. "But what are you talking about?"

"The first time we all went over, the day you came to talk about listing the house, Gloria said that they had both been at home at the time of Sally's murder. But when Ruby and I spoke to Don on Monday, he said that Gloria was home alone and called him at work when she heard the sirens," Connie said

"People lie all the time to cover for each other and avoid being suspects," Elyse said. "It's wrong, but that doesn't necessarily mean they are guilty of murder."

"You're right," Connie said. "I guess Don was just trying to protect his wife, but since they both have alibis for Amy's accident anyway, they're both off the hook.

Chapter 16

BY THE TIME Connie got home from her girls' night out, it was past midnight. Apparently, Stephanie had texted Grace to let her mother know about the late night, because when Connie got home, there was a handwritten note taped to her door that read, "Take your time coming in tomorrow morning. I heard it was a late night."

Thank you, Stephanie and Grace.

Connie dropped into bed, and the next thing she knew, her phone alarm was going off at 8:30 the next morning. Forgetting that Grace had agreed to open the store so Connie could sleep in, she lept out of bed and raced toward the bathroom. When she remembered that she could take her time, she smiled and slowly made her way into the kitchen to heat up some water for tea and make a thick smoothie.

When her tea was ready, Connie took her breakfast, along with her most recent newsletter from *Feeding the Hungry*, the non-profit where she worked for twelve years, to her favorite reclining chair to catch up the organization's activities. Judging from the newsletter, it looked like *Feeding the Hungry* was continuing to expand. Connie was thrilled to see that her successor was carrying on many of the projects Connie had started, and she was also beginning new initiatives. Connie had been so worried about leaving behind her work to move to Sapphire Beach, but seeing *Feeding the Hungry* thrive made her realize she had nothing to worry about. God was taking care of everything. She was where she was supposed to be.

After a leisurely second cup of tea, Connie took a longer-than-usual shower, then brought Ginger for a walk along some of the side streets off Sapphire Beach Boulevard. The streets were lined with bungalows, much like Stephanie's and the one Zach was in the process of purchasing. Connie said a quick prayer that Zach's deal would go through. She had never seen him so excited about anything, and she had to admit, she liked that he was planting roots in Sapphire Beach.

By the time Connie arrived at *Just Jewelry*, it was 10:30. She brought a large latte to thank Grace for opening the store alone.

"It was so nice to have part of the morning to myself," Connie said. "It got me thinking that I should go ahead and hire another part-time employee. I looked over the books the other day, and we can easily afford to hire another person."

"That's a smart move," Grace said. "You need a day off, and you shouldn't be in the store from opening to closing so many days in a row."

"It is starting to wear on me," Connie said. "I was hesitant to hire too many employees at first, but now that we've been open for almost a year, I feel confident that we can afford it."

The flyers that Connie and Abby had made about the Saturday morning jewelry-making class beginning in March had paid off. Connie had a group of ten students signed up, either via her online registration form or by stopping by the store. She was sitting at the oak table between customers preparing an email to send to the new class with some preliminary information, when two enthusiastic women bounded into the store.

"Good afternoon," Connie said, standing to greet them. "Welcome to *Just Jewelry*. Is there anything particular I can help you find?"

"My grandmother's friend recommended I stop by," one of the women said. "I'm getting married in June and was looking for someone to make custom jewelry for me and my bridesmaids."

"And, of course, for her stellar Maid of Honor," the other women said.

"Of course," the first woman said. "My name is Kristin, and this is my sister and Maid of Honor, Heather."

Connie took a deep breath. Taking this job would add a lot of work to her already hectic schedule, but how could she refuse? Creating custom jewelry for one of the most important days of someone's life was a privilege, and she had hoped her business would grow in this direction. However, having created the jewelry for her best friend, Bethany's, bridal party, Connie knew well the time commitment she was undertaking. Was she biting off more than she could chew?

Fortunately, Connie's doubts quickly disappeared. Connie and Kristin spent the next hour looking through magazines and photos of the bride's dress and bridesmaids' dresses until Connie was certain she knew exactly what the bride-to-be desired. Since she would need to get started immediately in order to give each piece the time and attention it deserved, Connie made sure to have all her ducks in a row before Kristin and Heather left.

When they finished, Kristin left a deposit and officially commissioned Connie. She was thrilled to have her first official wedding project.

Connie was so excited, that as soon as she had a few spare minutes, she called her mother's cell. She was hoping to catch both her mother, Jo, and sister, Gianna together, since they were often together working on their home staging business.

"Hi, honey, is everything okay?" her mother asked when she answered the phone. Connie usually waited until the evening to call home when she could talk with her father, as well.

"Hi Mom, yes, everything's fine. I just wanted to share some good news. Is Gi with you?"

"She's right here. I'll put you on speaker."

"Hi Connie," Gianna said.

Connie smiled when she heard her sister's voice.

"Is this wedding news?" Jo asked.

It took Connie a few seconds to realize what her mother was asking.

"Stop that, Mom," Gianna said, "Connie and Zach have only been on a few dates."

"Oh, I know," Jo said. "But a mother can dream."

"This has nothing to do with *my* wedding, but ironically, it *is* wedding news." Connie explained about being commissioned to make the jewelry for a bridal party for a June wedding.

"That's great!" Gianna said. "You're going to do an amazing job. I want to see pictures when they are done."

Jo agreed. "That's a big step in your business. I'm sure once you do one wedding, you're going to be in high demand."

Connie hadn't thought of that. If that did turn out to be the case, she would definitely need to hire more help.

Connie decided not to tell them about the murder investigation, since she didn't have time to get into the details, and she didn't want her family worrying. Before hanging up, Connie spent a few minutes running Zach's choice of finishes for his new home past Jo and Gianna. Her mother's and sister's ability to put together a room had rubbed off on Connie over the years, so she was confident in her interior design skills, but she always felt better running any major design decisions past the pros in the family.

"Those sound like beautiful choices," her mother said. "When Zach officially owns the house, don't forget to give us his new address so we can send him a congratulations card."

"I promise," Connie said. "I'd better go. I see a group of customers heading into my store, and I'm working alone until Abby gets here."

Later that afternoon, Connie was surprised to see Pamela come into her store.

"Pamela, it's nice to see you. Thanks for coming by *Just Jewelry*." But judging from the sense of purpose in her stride, Connie didn't think she had come to shop.

"I'm sorry to interrupt you at work, but I was hoping we could talk for a few minutes," Pamela said.

"Absolutely. Just give me a couple of minutes with these customers and I'll be right with you." Connie gestured toward the sofa. "Why don't you have a seat and make yourself comfortable. I shouldn't be too long."

Connie finished helping a couple of customers and took payment from a woman who had purchased a birthday gift for her niece. Then she joined Pamela on the sofa.

Pamela was bouncing her knee and staring nervously out the window.

"You seem agitated. Is everything okay?" Connie asked.

"I'm sorry to bother you," Pamela blurted out. "I didn't know where else to go."

"Did something happen?" Connie asked.

"Not exactly," Pamela said. "It's about some information I came across. Do you remember how Jack was in a sour mood when you came by the food bank on Monday?" Pamela asked.

Connie nodded. How could she forget that awkward trip to her car where he wouldn't even look at her?

"Now I know why," Pamela said. "I overheard a conversation between Kyle and Jack. Apparently, Jack borrowed a friend's car over the weekend and got into an accident. Kyle paid for the damages and is making Jack work it off at the food bank."

"Do you know exactly when he borrowed his friend's car?"

"Friday night, the same night that Amy was in the accident. And that's not all," Pamela said. "The car that Jack had the accident with is black, the same color as the car that drove Amy off the road."

Chapter 17

"THAT'S HUGE," Connie said. "That means there's a good chance Jack is the killer. We have to tell the police."

"I was on my way to the police station after I found out, but then I got scared, so I came here instead. What if Kyle and Jack find out it was me who told the police? What if they hurt me before the police can arrest them? I have to work with them, and I can't afford to quit my job."

"If you can wait until after 4:00, when my employee is due to arrive, I can go with you to the police station. Try not to worry, the police won't let anything happen to you."

As soon as Abby arrived, Connie took Pamela to the Sapphire Beach Police Station so she could tell them what she heard. Connie had texted Josh in advance, so he was waiting for Pamela when they arrived. While Connie was waiting for Pamela, Zach came into the waiting room.

"I heard you were out here," he said, giving her a warm smile.

"I'm waiting for Pamela. We came, because she overheard a conversation that could help with the investigation into Sally Boyd's murder."

"We could use a fresh lead in that case about now," he said. "But on another note, I'm glad you're here. I was going to call you tonight. Our Valentine's date…"

"The one I know nothing about," Connie interrupted.

Zach winked at her. "Yes, that one. Anyway, it really should be in the daylight, so I was hoping I could pick you up earlier than we talked about. 3:30 would be perfect."

"It shouldn't be a problem. I just have to get coverage for the store."

"I already ran it by Grace, and she enthusiastically agreed stay until Abby arrives at 4:00 so you can leave early."

Connie had to laugh. "You thought of everything. In that case, I'll see you at 3:30."

"Perfect," he said. "And don't eat a big lunch. Our date will include an early dinner."

"Are you even going to give me a hint about what we're doing?"

"With *your* detective skills? Not a chance," he said. "I'd better get back to work. I'll see you tomorrow."

"See you tomorrow. I'm looking forward to it. I *think*."

About a half hour later, Pamela was finished, so Connie drove her back to *Just Jewelry* to get her car. Pamela appeared less anxious on the ride home. According to Pamela, Josh assured her that he would protect her identity.

As soon as Pamela left, Connie went next door to Ruby's shop to tell her the good news.

"So, it's over?" Ruby asked. "Jack is the killer?"

"I wouldn't go that far. The police haven't made an arrest, but if Jack was in a car accident last Friday with his friend's black car, and Amy was run off the road by a black car, it seems to me that it's only a matter of time before they gather enough evidence to arrest him."

"So, it turns out that Jack knew that Sally had incriminating information against his father and decided to take matters into his own hands?" Ruby said.

"It appears that way."

"I wonder what this will mean for the food bank," Ruby said.

That concern weighed heavily on Connie's heart, as well. "Hopefully, Kyle will do the right thing and resign before he gets fired and brings even more negative publicity on Community Food Bank. That way they can move past this dark chapter. It's unfortunate, but at least it's out of our hands. It's up to the police to investigate Jack and make an arrest."

Throughout the rest of Wednesday and Thursday, Connie couldn't help but wonder why Zach had insisted on an early dinner on Valentine's Day. It seemed like a strange request. When Friday finally arrived, Connie left work at 2:30 to get ready for her date. She showered and was ready to go well before Zach arrived with a dozen red roses in hand. He was anxious to get going, so as soon as Connie put the flowers in water and Zach said a quick hello to Ginger, they headed out.

"You're still not going to tell me where we're going?" Connie asked, as they took a right onto Sapphire Beach Boulevard, which was in the opposite direction from downtown.

He shook his head. "Not yet, but we're almost there."

After traveling about a quarter of a mile down the boulevard, Zach took a left onto a side street, then another left, never leaving the residential neighborhoods. The brightly colored bungalows made Connie feel like she was on vacation, even though she was less than a half mile from home. Many of the homes featured mailboxes in the form of sea creatures. There were dolphins, manatees, surfboards, and the occasional mermaid.

Zach had told Connie that their date would include dinner, but there were no restaurants in sight. She considered that maybe he was taking her on a picnic, but there were no public parks or beaches on this side of the boulevard.

She looked at Zach, wondering where they were going. Was he taking her for a drive by his soon-to-be house before dinner?

The next thing she knew, Zach was pulling into the driveway of a tired looking bungalow with chipped blue paint and weathered white shutters. He turned off the engine to his Jeep and looked at Connie expectantly.

"Is this your new house?" she asked.

"You guessed it," he said, meeting her by the passenger-side door. "I closed on the house this morning, a week early, and just got the keys. I wanted to surprise you."

Zach looked like a little boy on Christmas morning. He took Connie's hand and led her around back to the lanai, which was set against the backdrop of a canal. There was a set of patio furniture that looked brand new in contrast to the cracked tile floor beneath it.

"If you think the outside of the house looks bad," he said, "wait until you see the inside. It's a complete disaster." Even as he described the dilapidated state of the house, his eyes danced with excitement.

"It looks like the boat lift is new," Connie said, looking for a silver lining.

"Thank God for small miracles," Zach said. "It's about the only thing."

Zach motioned toward a large royal blue cooler in the corner of the lanai. "I took the day off today for the closing and for the delivery of the patio furniture, so I made dinner at my apartment and brought it over just before I picked you up. When I give you the grand tour, you'll see why I didn't want to leave it in the refrigerator."

There was also a bottle of Chardonnay chilling in an ice bucket and two wine glasses on the table, placed in front of a tall vase with another dozen red roses.

"I ordered the furniture before I even bought the house, because I wanted to make sure it was delivered in time for our date," Zach said, slipping his arms around her waist. "I wanted you to be a part of the first memory I make in my new home."

She smiled and kissed him. "Thank you, Zach. I'm so happy to be sharing this day with you."

"Dinner will keep a little longer. Come," he said guiding her toward the sliding door that led into the house. "I can't wait to show you."

It took some effort to pull it open, but they entered the living room through a glass sliding door. "I'll need to replace this slider, as well as all the other windows. The heating and air conditioning system is new, and the roof is only five years old, but other than that, everything else will need to be replaced."

Connie scanned the living area. It was an open concept space, with a good sized living room and an area in front of the kitchen for a dining table. The little house had good bones, but Zach had not been exaggerating about its rough condition. Several of the blue ceramic tiles that ran throughout the house were cracked, and the walls looked like they hadn't been painted since the house was built. The faint smell of stale cigarette smoke hung in the air. Connie hoped that it would go away by the time Zach finished the renovations.

Connie followed Zach into the kitchen, where the door to one of the cabinets looked as if it had been chewed by a dog and the laminate countertops were separating from the sides of the counter. The white appliances were dented and covered in grime. "Now you can see why I didn't want to cook dinner here."

"Good decision," Connie said after peeking inside the dirty, rusty refrigerator

Zach was undeterred. "Everything you can see will be replaced. The house has three bedrooms and one bathroom and is about 1,100 square feet total, plus the outdoor area, where I imagine I'll be spending a lot of my time."

Zach started talking a mile a minute, and his chatter warmed Connie's heart. She had never seen him this excited about anything. "I'm going to demolish everything until the house is only a shell, then replace it with all the finishes we chose." Connie thought of the tiles that resembled wood, the warm gray paint, and the white cabinets. She was beginning to catch Zach's vision. "I'll put a coat of Kilz primer on the walls to get rid of the smell, and everything will feel brand new."

"Are you keeping your apartment while you do the work?" Connie couldn't imagine him living here in this condition, but she knew he wasn't afraid to rough it.

"I have my apartment until April 1, so that's roughly another six weeks. I'll be moving in then no matter what condition it's in. I'm taking next week off from work to get started, and I have some friends coming by weekends and evenings to help me out. Of course, I'll hire professionals for a lot of it, but I'll do what I can myself. I'm hoping it will be livable by April 1 but worst-case scenario, it will be like camping for a while."

"You're not wasting any time," Connie said.

"Not a second. As soon as the dumpster is delivered tomorrow morning, I start demolition."

"I can't wait to see the finished product," Connie said. "It's going to be amazing."

When they returned to the lanai, Connie looked back at the train wreck of a house Zach had just bought and smiled. He had a lot of work ahead of him, but he also had enthusiasm to spare.

It was a beautiful evening, and Zach had outdone himself on the simple but delicious meal. They each had a salad with mixed greens, followed by salmon, rice, and asparagus, which Zach heated up in a small microwave he brought for the occasion, and also to have on hand to heat future lunches at the worksite.

For dessert, he brought them each a double fudge chocolate cupcake.

As they finished their dessert, the sun was setting, turning the sky bright orange behind the dark water. Zach had timed dinner perfectly. In the dim light of dusk, the little blue bungalow with chipped paint and overgrown landscaping looked perfect. It *was* perfect.

Chapter 18

CONNIE AND ZACH sipped their wine and talked until darkness descended and the temperature dropped. Then they cleaned up the patio and Zach drove Connie home.

"It's still early," he said as they pulled into the long driveway leading to Palm Paradise, flanked with coconut palms. "Would you like to go for a walk on the beach?"

"I would love to," Connie said. "Plus, it won't hurt to work off some of that double fudge cupcake - even though it was worth every bite."

They took the walkway that lead around Palm Paradise and strolled past the pool and toward the Gulf. Then they walked hand-in-hand along hard, cool sand in the direction of the pier. The full moon cast its beams on the dark waters below. It was cool but comfortable enough, as long as they kept moving.

Zach looked out toward the waters, illuminated by moonlight. "I always feel so small standing next to the vast ocean."

"I know what you mean," Connie said. "It's a comforting feeling to know that some things are bigger than we are and that there's order to the world, even if I don't always understand that order." Connie couldn't help but think of the senseless act of violence that took Sally's life. "When nothing seems to make sense, I find comfort in the immensity of nature."

Zach looked at her thoughtfully and nodded.

They got about halfway to the pier, which was a mile from Connie's condo, and turned around.

"Speaking of making sense out of things, was Pamela's statement helpful to the investigation into Sally's death?" Connie asked.

"Ah, yes. I've been so busy with my house that it nearly slipped my mind that you once again find yourself connected to a murder investigation."

"Small town living, I guess. Ruby is a good neighbor, and she and Grace have become great friends since I opened the shop."

Zach gazed ahead into the distance for a moment, then back at Connie. "Tell me, what do you know about Kyle and his son Jack from your investigations?"

Connie collected her thoughts. "I know that Kyle is the CFO of Community Food Bank and that Jack is a college student who volunteers there a lot. Apparently, Sally was helping Kyle out with an administrative project and came across some information on his computer that indicated he might be embezzling money from the food bank. Kyle must have seen what Sally was looking at on his computer, because he immediately escorted her out of his office and back to the sorting room, where the other volunteers were working. It seems Kyle never requested Sally's help again. But Sally must have managed to email herself the documents or snap pictures of them with her phone, because she had a printout of the budgets for the last five years in her home office. My guess is that since Sally had done so many successful fundraisers, she was disturbed to see that the budgets indicated donations were down. She probably suspected that somebody, probably Kyle, was embezzling, and Kyle was afraid her discovery would open an investigation into his activities."

Zach arched his eyebrows. "Very impressive. If you're ever looking to change fields, we could use your skills and keen sense of justice at the station," he said playfully.

"No, thank you," Connie said. "I'll stick to making jewelry and running a small business. Those activities provide me with enough safer problems to solve."

Zach laughed. "Fair enough. I forgot that it was you and Ruby who found the budget printouts at Sally's." He hesitated for a brief moment. "I suppose it will be public information soon enough. It turns out that Kyle was indeed embezzling money from the food bank, and Jack knew about it. Jack admitted to having a gambling debt that was getting out of hand and Kyle…"

"Let me guess," Connie interrupted. "Out of desperation, Kyle began skimming money from the various fundraising efforts of the food bank, including the income from Sally's fundraisers. So, when Sally saw the budget, she knew the numbers looked off, since she knew how much money she had raised."

"You got it."

"And Jack either knew that Kyle killed Sally, or he simply knew that Kyle had 'borrowed' money from the food bank to pay off Jack's debts, so he killed Sally to protect his father's reputation."

"That part still remains to be seen," Zach said. "Kyle and Jack are both denying that either of them killed Sally. Jack admitted to driving Amy off the road, but he said he didn't intend to hurt her. He just wanted to scare you, Ruby, and Grace away from investigating so that his father's activities wouldn't come to light. He thought that if you believed that Amy's life was in danger, you'd stop asking questions."

"How did Jack know that Amy was Ruby's niece?"

"He said he overheard a conversation about it when you and Ruby were volunteering at the food bank."

"Come to think of it, Jack could have been lurking around when Ruby and I were talking to some of the other volunteers about Amy. Ruby was saying how happy she was to have Amy in her life, and that we wanted to figure out who the killer was and clear Amy's name."

"That must be what gave Jack the idea that if he could stop you from investigating Sally's murder, you wouldn't ask any more questions about the missing money from the food bank," Zach said.

"Ironically, it had the opposite effect. Since Amy's accident, Ruby has been more determined than ever to find the killer so that Amy would feel safe," Connie said.

"He obviously didn't think it through. I think it was a panicked decision."

"Do you believe Jack? Do you think the killer isn't the same person who ran Amy off the road?" Connie asked.

"We're still investigating, but there is no evidence yet to suggest Jack killed Sally. Both Jack and Kyle have a motive – Kyle's being his apparent embezzlement and Jack's to protect his father. I'm not convinced they're both innocent, but we have no evidence against either of them."

They walked in silence the rest of the way back to Palm Paradise. Connie wondered how the staff at the food bank was handling this news. It must be devastating for them. Connie knew from her own work how one bad apple could spoil the bushel and hinder the important work of an organization.

Zach walked Connie into the lobby after they stopped by his car to get the roses that Zach had used to decorate the table at dinner. "I start demolition bright and early tomorrow morning, so I'm going to make it an early night."

"Thank you for the wonderful Valentine's date," Connie said. "And for the flowers."

He smiled. "I hope it's the first of many," he said. Then he kissed her and left.

Connie was on cloud nine after her date, especially because Zach wanted to share his first memory in his new home with her. She hoped it would be the first of many, as well.

After Zach left, Connie took Ginger for a walk, then settled on her sofa with her dog curled up next to her, thinking about her conversation with Zach about the investigation. Her thoughts went to Pamela and the rest of the staff at Community Food Bank.

She wondered how much they knew about what Kyle and Jack did.

Remembering that she had Pamela's business card from the wake, she retrieved it from her wallet. It was nearly 8:30 on Valentine's Day, so maybe it wasn't the best time to call. But she ignored that thought and called anyway.

Pamela's tired voice came through the phone. "Hello."

"Hi Pamela, it's Connie. I hope I'm not interrupting your Valentine's Day celebration, but I heard what happened earlier today and just wanted to see how you were doing."

"Thank you for calling, Connie. After the day I've had, my husband agreed to move our celebration to tomorrow. I think he is secretly happy for the postponement, because he's always complaining that restaurants jack up their prices on Valentine's Day and New Year's Eve."

"So, how are things at the food bank? I heard the police were there today."

"It's been a crazy day. The entire staff has been in meetings all day with the Board of Directors formulating a plan. To Kyle's credit, in order to spare the food bank any negative publicity, he has agreed to resign quietly and promised to pay back the money he took. He looked truly broken and desperate. As wrong as his decision was, I felt bad for him. I don't think he killed Sally."

"I'm glad to hear that Kyle's cooperating," Connie said.

"The Board of Directors named our current Programs Manager as the new CFO, and they asked me to become the new Program Director."

"Oh, Pamela, I'm so happy. They couldn't have made a better choice."

"Do you think so?" Pamela asked.

"Absolutely. I remember the tour you gave the first time I came to the food bank. Your passion for the mission is evident."

"Thank you. I'm very excited about this opportunity, even if it came from a less-than-perfect reason. Connie, I really hope you can find the killer so we can put this behind us once and for all. Everyone here will breathe easier when we know the killer is behind bars."

Connie let out a disappointed sigh. She had hoped that, after discovering that Jack was the one who hit

Amy's car, the mystery would be wrapped up. But here it was, three weeks after Sally's murder, and Connie still had just as many questions. All of her original suspects, including Tammy, whom she had ruled out when she assumed it was the killer who caused Amy's accident, were now back in the running. The killer could be *any* of her initial suspects – Tammy, Kyle, Jack, Patsy, Don, or Gloria.

Chapter 19

AFTER TALKING TO PAMELA, Connie was wound up. Since it was still early, she texted Grace to see if she was busy.

Come on over, came Grace's immediate reply. *I'll put on some water for hot chocolate.*

A few minutes later, Connie was next door at Grace's apartment sipping a warm cup of sweetness.

Grace's home had a nearly identical layout to Connie's, except it was the mirror image. It had an open concept living space between the kitchen, living room, and dining room, with the master bedroom suite on one side and a smaller guest suite on the other. Grace's condo had more of a country-farmhouse décor, while Connie's style was a bit more eclectic, with elegant pieces of furniture she inherited from her aunt, alongside pictures, vases, and other items from Connie's travels, especially throughout Africa.

"So, how was your date with Zach?" Grace asked.

"It was wonderful," Connie said. "Thanks again for covering for me at work."

"Zach was so sweet when he called me to ask if I could work a few extra hours so he could take you out on Valentine's Day. He really likes you."

Connie felt her cheeks grow warm. "The feeling is mutual. I'm enjoying getting to know him."

"What do you mean, 'getting to know him?'" Grace asked. "You've known each other for over a year now. In my day, that was enough to know all you needed to know."

Connie laughed. "You sound like my mother. We met over a year ago, but we've still only been on a few dates. I love that you like Zach, but I'm just starting a business and a new life, and Zach just bought the fixer upper of his dreams. As much as I like him, I'm good taking it slowly."

After answering the rest of Grace's enthusiastic questions about her date with Zach, Connie updated

Grace on her conversation with Pamela and what was going on at Community Food Bank.

"The bottom line," Connie said, after explaining the situation, "is that Jack is the one who caused Amy's car accident, but there is no evidence that he or his father killed Sally."

"So, that means we're back to square one," Grace said. "Poor Ruby. She is so anxious to put this whole thing behind her."

"I know," Connie said. "And the worst part is that Tammy is now back on the list of suspects."

"Along with Kyle and Jack, who still could be guilty, and Patsy, Don, and Gloria," Grace said.

"I think Patsy is unlikely, because she would have to have killed Sally and then called an Uber to take her home."

"Unless she had an accomplice who was driving," Grace said.

"But it couldn't have been Tim. He had no motive. It's not believable that she would find a friend to help her kill a romantic rival. That would be one deranged friend. And, anyway, the murder wasn't premeditated, because the killer used Sally's

195

lamp as the murder weapon. It just doesn't seem likely."

"That leaves Tammy, Jack, Kyle, Don, and Gloria," Grace said.

"Tammy's album *was* at Sally's, after she lied about not being there, but Jack and Kyle had the strongest motive," Connie said.

"Don't forget that Gloria has two conflicting alibis. If Don was at work, he has an alibi, but if he was at home with Gloria, one could be covering for the other," Grace said.

"Or Gloria could have done it while Don was at work," Connie added.

"After my shift at *Just Jewelry* tomorrow, I'll take Ruby to lunch and update her on what's going on," Grace said.

"That's probably a good idea. I don't envy you that task."

After they finished their hot chocolate, Connie went home. Since she was too restless to sleep, she decided to do a few household chores. Forty minutes later, the dishwasher was emptied, the floors were clean, and there was a load of clothes tumbling in the dryer, but she was still too restless to sleep. She settled into her living room sofa with Ginger on her lap and surfed the television channels, until she settled on a Valentine's Day romance movie that she hoped would take her mind of the case.

And it did… for a couple of hours. But within a few minutes of the happy ending, which made her feel like all was right with the world, Connie was bouncing her knee, and her thoughts had drifted back to the murder investigation. All was *not* right with the world as long as Sally's killer was walking the streets of Sapphire Beach, and Ruby and Amy were kept apart.

"What am I missing, girl?" Connie asked Ginger, who lifted her head momentarily, then dropped it back on Connie's lap, as if commiserating with Connie's predicament.

Connie doubted there could be another person whom she hadn't yet discovered with a reason to want Sally dead. She had talked to too many people who knew Sally well. Somebody would have known if Sally had another enemy.

She thought about how ironic it was that Kevin used to be a federal prosecutor before he met Sally, and Sally would be the one to discover the discrepancies in the food bank's budget. If Kevin had still been alive, he would have been able to help Sally handle the situation. Too bad the final weeks of her life had to be filled with so much stress.

Then she had a thought. As a federal prosecutor, Kevin probably had a lot of enemies. Could whoever killed Sally have been seeking revenge for something Kevin did? She quickly dismissed that idea. It seemed unlikely, especially since Kevin was no longer alive.

Still, just out of curiosity, Connie decided to do an internet search. She typed 'Kevin Boyd federal prosecutor' into the search engine, and a bunch of articles about his cases came up. She started reading a few, but all it did was make her tired and frustrated. It was like looking for a needle in a haystack, when she wasn't even sure the needle *was* in the haystack. Finally, she closed her laptop and went to bed.

The next morning, Connie woke up before her alarm went off and she found herself ready for work early. She took Ginger for an extra-long walk along the boulevard to give her plenty of exercise before a busy Saturday in the shop, then they got in the car and made the one-mile commute downtown. Since

Connie was early, she stopped to pick up a coffee for her and Grace and got the shop ready to open.

It was another busy February Saturday in downtown Sapphire Beach, and the day flew by. Grace was working until 1:00 and Abby would be coming in at 4:00 for the night shift, so fortunately Connie wouldn't have to handle the weekend crowds alone.

Grace finished checking out a customer at 1:00 and went over to Ruby's shop next door to invite Ruby to lunch. She wanted to update her on the situation at Community Food Bank. A few minutes later, Grace came back to *Just Jewelry* alone.

"Where's Ruby?" Connie asked.

"One of her employees told me that she took the day off to finish cleaning out Sally's house. I texted Ruby to offer my help, but she said there was no need for me to come. Since her ankle is healed, she is making quick work of it. She said she only needs to finish packing the kitchen and do some light cleaning. If she needs any help loading the last of the boxes into her car, her neighbor, Don Higgins, offered to help."

"That's right," Connie said. "I remember him offering the last time I was there helping her. I'm sure she'll be fine. Ruby is right. You should take a day to yourself. Between working extra hours, helping Ruby, and the investigation, you've been on the go nonstop."

Grace smiled. "Maybe you're right. To be honest, I wouldn't mind taking a book to the beach and getting lost in a good mystery novel."

Connie turned to get something out back and then suddenly froze.

"What's the matter?" Grace asked.

"Did you say Don Higgins was going to help Ruby? *Donald* Higgins?"

"Yes, Don, the neighbor we met. Why do you ask?"

Connie went behind the circular counter in the middle of the store and pulled her laptop computer from one of the shelves. She put it on the counter and did the same internet search she had done the night before. A few links down, she found the article she was looking for.

"Read this article," Connie said, pushing the computer in front of Grace.

When she got to the end of the article, Grace looked nervously at Connie. "Do you think the Donald Higgins in this article is the man who lives next door to Sally's house?"

"If it is, then Kevin Boyd prosecuted him twenty-five years ago for tax fraud and cost him a huge amount in fines. If he's still holding a grudge, he could be Sally's killer."

"We have to get to Sally's house to make sure Ruby isn't alone with him," Grace said.

"We can't *both* go. Why don't you stay here and watch the store and I'll stop by. We might be worrying for no reason."

"Okay," Grace said reluctantly. "But call me as soon as you get there."

Chapter 20

CONNIE RACED to the parking lot down the street and got into her car. She took a sharp left onto Sapphire Beach Boulevard, causing an oncoming driver to hit his brakes and honk. She halfheartedly waved an apology and sped toward Sally's house, her anxiety mounting at each turn.

Ruby *had* to be okay.

The five-minute drive felt like a half hour, but soon Connie was pulling her Jetta onto Sally's street and parking a short distance from the house. She quickly exited the car, closing the door quietly in case she needed to enter the house undetected. As she approached Sally's house, she tried to convince herself that Ruby was fine. The odds of her being in danger were next to nothing. But Connie's heart still felt like it was beating through her chest as she tiptoed across the front walkway and crouched down beside the large double window outside Sally's living room. She slowly raised herself up and peeked inside. There was only Ruby, singing as she ran a dust mop over the tile floors.

Connie's whole body relaxed in relief when she saw Ruby's cheerful expression.

The front door was unlocked, so Connie entered the house and called Ruby's name. When she didn't answer, Connie called her name again louder. Still no response. Then she saw the white wire coming from Ruby's ears and realized she was wearing earbuds. When she approached Ruby and gently tapped her on the shoulder, Ruby jumped back a few feet, almost knocking Connie over.

"Oh, my goodness, you scared me, Connie! What on earth are you doing here?"

"I didn't mean to startle you. Grace went to your shop to see if you wanted to go out to lunch, and one of your employees told her you were here. I'm so glad you're alone. I have something important to tell you."

"But I'm..." Ruby started to say, but Connie raised her hand, signaling for Ruby to stop talking.

"Ruby, this is important. Just let me say it." Connie glanced out the back slider window toward Don's and Gloria's house, but there was no sign of either of them. She quickly explained about how Kevin, during his time as a federal prosecutor, prosecuted Don for tax fraud, forcing him to pay a small fortune in back taxes and penalties.

Ruby looked horrified.

"I'll tell you more once we get out of here," Connie said. "I just came over to make sure you were safe. We need to go straight to the police."

Suddenly, a loud crash came from the direction of the hallway.

Connie jerked her head toward the noise and her heart skipped a beat when her eyes met Don's angry glare. He had slammed two boxes on the floor in front of him.

Don grabbed Ruby and dragged her in the direction of the kitchen, which was a few feet away. "Nobody is going anywhere!" he said, snatching a butcher knife that was on the counter and holding it by Ruby's throat.

Why did we have to wait to pack up the kitchen last?! Connie thought.

"Let go of me," Ruby cried. "You're hurting my ankle." Ruby turned her head to try to face Don. "*You* killed Sally?"

Connie tried to inch closer. She knew Ruby's ankle wasn't fully healed, and she wouldn't be able to outrun Don, even if Connie could knock the knife away. So, she tried to buy time by talking while she thought of another plan.

"Don and your brother, Kevin, go way back, isn't that right Don? But I'm guessing he didn't kill Sally to get revenge on Kevin, or he would have taken his revenge a long time ago." Connie looked squarely at Don. "You did it because of the garage, didn't you? Sally was insisting you tear it down and, as you said yourself, you couldn't afford to tear it down, then build another, smaller one."

"For years, Gloria and I watched Kevin and Sally spend their vacations enjoying this house. Their *second* home was nicer than our primary residence, thanks to what Kevin did to me. He came after me ruthlessly, and I lost everything. At this point in my life, I should be living the high life, not struggling financially. And to top it off, Kevin never even recognized me. All those years, Kevin and Sally waved at us from their lanai, acting like friendly neighbors, and they didn't even know who we were."

"The garage was the last straw, wasn't it?" Connie asked.

"We saved up for years to build that garage. I wasn't going to let Sally deliver my family another financial blow after all this time."

While Don was talking, Ruby motioned with her eyes toward the wall on the other side of the kitchen.

"I went over to reason with Sally," Don continued. "I wasn't planning to kill her, but she refused to listen."

Don looked away for a split second, so Connie glanced in the direction that Ruby had indicated and saw that Ruby's crutches were resting against the wall.

Stalling, Connie said, "It wasn't you who drove Amy off the road, was it?"

"That stupid kid," Don said with a careless laugh. "I thought for sure I was off the hook when he caused that girl's accident."

As Don was speaking, Connie thought she detected movement coming from the lanai. She tried to catch a glimpse of who it might be, but Don was in the way. Suddenly, the screen door to the lanai opened, and Gloria's voice carried into the house. "Don, what's taking you so long? We're going to be late."

Don looked behind him. "Gloria, stay back! I'm not finished here."

As he turned around, Connie made a mad dash for one of the crutches, while Ruby stomped on the top of Don's foot.

"Ouch, my bad ankle," Ruby cried. "I should have used the other foot."

While Don bent over in pain, Connie swung the crutch, whacking him with the handle and knocking him to the ground. As Don fell, he dropped the knife, and Ruby slid it across the room with her foot.

Gloria, apparently not comprehending that Don was trying to harm Ruby and Connie, shouted, "Why did you hit my husband?! I'm calling the police!"

But as soon as the words left Gloria's mouth, there was a thunderous knock at the front door. "It's the police. Open up!"

Connie sprinted to open the door, and in came a deputy officer followed by Josh, about five seconds behind.

Chapter 21

GLORIA TENDERLY helped Don up from the floor, apparently still not comprehending what had just happened. She still seemed convinced Don was the victim.

"How did you know to come?" Connie asked Josh.

"Grace called and filled me in. She was trying to reach the two of you to make sure everything was okay, but when neither one of you responded, she called me. Luckily, I'm working today, following up on leads for this case. Deputy Peterson was patrolling the area, and I wasn't that far away either, so we both came."

Connie and Ruby recounted everything that happened, beginning with the garage fiasco and the articles she found about Don and Kevin's history, then ending with Don pulling the knife on Ruby and admitting to killing Sally.

"That can't be true," Gloria said. "Don wouldn't hurt a fly."

Connie's heart went out to Gloria. She got hit with a lot of shocking information in a matter of a few minutes, and it appeared that she had been completely in the dark about her husband's guilt.

Deputy Peterson took Don and Gloria to the police station, while Josh taped the crime scene so the forensics team could do its job. Then Connie and Ruby both followed Josh to the police station to give their official statements.

Connie called Grace while they were on their way to let her know she would be a little longer than anticipated.

By the time they finished at the police station and returned to *Just Jewelry*, Abby had just arrived for her shift.

Grace gave Connie and Ruby a warm hug the second they walked through the door. "What am I going to do with you two? You took ten years off my life this afternoon."

"It was a horrible afternoon," Ruby said. "But at least we can finally put this whole nightmare behind us." In between helping customers, Connie and Ruby filled Grace and Abby in on everything that had happened.

"I guess I was right to insist that you keep your crutches close by in case of an emergency," Grace said to Ruby in a slightly horrified tone. "I just didn't anticipate that the emergency would involve defending yourself from a murderer wielding a knife."

"I'm just so glad it's over," Ruby said. "I can't wait to call Amy and tell her that she is no longer in danger. I hope and pray that Jody will change her mind about Amy meeting the rest of the family."

"I can't see why she wouldn't," Connie said. "But before you call Amy, promise me you'll get off your feet and ice that ankle, or you'll be needing those crutches again."

"I'd better do that," Ruby said. "Especially since my crutches are now evidence. I have a feeling I would have a hard time explaining *that* to my insurance company if I needed to request another pair."

213

"I think I'm going to call it a day, too," Grace said. "There's a lounge chair in the sunshine and a mystery novel calling my name."

"Can you hold on for just a minute?" Abby asked. "I have some news I'd like to share."

The store was empty, so Connie and Grace sat on the sofa while Abby sat in of the armchairs facing them. Judging from Abby's smile, it was good news.

"In all the excitement today, I almost forgot to tell you that I got accepted into the PhD program at Florida Sands University. I'll officially be studying American Literature in southwest Florida for the next several years!"

Connie let out a squeal and hugged Abby. "Congratulations, Abby. I'm so proud of you. And I'm thrilled that you'll be with us at *Just Jewelry* for the foreseeable future."

"That's worth celebrating," Grace said. "I'll bring a cake tomorrow, and we can have a little celebration."

As Connie and Grace finished congratulating Abby, a wave of customers came into the store.

"I'll let you two handle this," Grace said. "I'm exhausted."

***

The following Saturday, Connie knocked on Grace's door to see if she was ready to leave. Ruby had invited them both to her home for dinner so they could be there when Ruby introduced Amy to the rest of the family. Because they knew Ruby was nervous, Connie and Grace agreed to arrive a little early to help her set up.

Grace answered the door, carrying a Tupperware container filled with what looked like homemade vanilla ice cream.

"Did you make ice cream to bring to Ruby's?" Connie asked, slightly confused, since it didn't look like enough for everyone.

"Not exactly. I used to make ice cream all the time for Concetta, Brenda, and myself. I can't tell you how many problems we solved on one of our balconies over a dish or two of ice cream. Concetta and I preferred strawberry, but vanilla was Brenda's favorite."

Connie smiled. "You made that for Brenda."

Grace's eyes grew misty. "Life is short, and I think it's time to put all this bitterness behind me and extend an olive branch to Brenda. Concetta would want it this way. Could you tell Ruby I had something to do, but that I'll be there in time for dinner?"

Connie gave Grace a quick hug. "Of course. Take your time. We'll see you when you get there."

When Connie arrived at Ruby's, there wasn't much work left to do. They opened the dining room table and set it for dinner, then hung tight and waited for everyone to arrive. Ruby was on cloud nine.

"I received some more good news today," Ruby said, while they waited. "Elyse called and told me that Gloria has agreed to have the garage taken down. Apparently, she couldn't bear to look at it, knowing all of the pain and suffering it had caused. As soon as the garage is removed, I'll be able to put Sally's house on the market."

"That's wonderful," Connie said.

"Not only that," Ruby said, "but now that Community Food Bank has replaced Kyle, it will be safe to donate some of the money from the sale of Sally's home to her favorite cause after all."

"With Pamela as the new Program Director, her final donation will be put to good use," Connie said.

Grace was the first to arrive, and judging from the broad smile she was wearing, her time with Brenda had gone well.

Tammy and her husband, Ray, arrived next, followed by Glen, and shortly after, Amy and Jody. Amy's fiancé, Peter, wasn't able to make it, so he promised he would come another time, but Ruby was thrilled that Jody had accepted her invitation.

Ruby's family warmly welcomed Amy over dinner, asking her so many questions about herself that Ruby had to slow them down so that Amy would have a chance to eat her dinner. Tammy and Glen were amazed at how much Amy reminded them of Kevin.

After dinner, Ruby directed everyone into the living room, where eight boxes were stacked against a wall.

"As I was going through Sally's belongings, I set aside some items for each of you that I thought you might like to remember her and Kevin by. I know we all had our issues with her, but over the past few weeks I've learned a lot about Sally that I wish I had known while she was alive, especially the way she tried to honor Kevin's memory through her volunteering. I thought that keeping some items that belonged to Sally and Kevin as mementos would help us all remember the good times."

Ruby sat next to Amy as she opened her box.

Tears rolled down Amy's cheek as she looked through a photo album that contained pictures of Kevin throughout his life.

"I made that especially for you," Ruby said. Then she handed her a jewelry box. "Here, open this."

Amy gasped when she opened the box, which contained a white gold necklace with a diamond heart pendant.

Ruby took Amy's hand. "I have a feeling Sally would have loved having you in her life, and if she had met you, she would have wanted you to have something nice to remember her by. Kevin bought this for her on her birthday the year before he died, and she cherished it. In a way, it's a gift from both Sally and your father."

Amy hugged Ruby, then Jody fastened the necklace around Amy's neck.

"Thank you for treating my daughter so kindly," Jody said.

"Don't be silly. She's family," Ruby said. "You both are."

Amidst everything that had happened, Ruby even found time to set some things aside for Connie and Grace. She gave Grace two silk scarfs she had admired at Sally's house, and Connie's box was filled with serving dishes, grilling accessories, and other kitchen supplies.

"Those are for Zach's new home," Ruby said. "I figured he would need them, since he's moving from a small apartment into a house and plans on entertaining a lot in his new space. Every little bit helps."

"Thank you, Ruby, that is so thoughtful. He can definitely use them."

"And this is for you," Ruby said, handing Connie a small container. "They are beads that I found in Sally's craft room. I was hoping you could create some jewelry to sell in your store and donate the proceeds to the food bank."

"What a great idea," Connie said. "I would be honored."

"And finally," Ruby said, "there's one more thing I'd like you to all have." Ruby handed each person a copy of a promotional magazine put out by Community Food Bank, which contained an in-depth article outlining Sally's journey to the food bank and the work she did in memory of Kevin. It included a wedding photo of Sally and Kevin, as well as other photos of Sally volunteering.

By the end of the evening, Ruby's family had made plans to get together again with Amy, and Ruby couldn't have been happier.

After everyone left, Connie and Grace stayed behind to help Ruby clean up. When the last dish was loaded into the dishwasher, the three women gathered around Ruby's kitchen island with a mug of tea.

"Tonight was special for so many reasons," Ruby said. "Seeing my family come together to honor Sally and welcome Amy reminded me of the special gift Kevin had for uniting the family. I can't help but feel that Amy inherited that same ability."

"It seems the lessons in forgiveness and unity have extended beyond your family," Grace said. She told Connie and Ruby all about her reconciliation with Brenda. "It feels wonderful to have my friend back."

"I never could have imagined last year when you moved into the shop next door that you would become such wonderful friends," Ruby said. "But tonight never could have happened without the two of you."

"That's worth drinking to," Connie said raising her mug. "To unexpected friendships."

"And to new beginnings," Ruby said.

Connie couldn't ask for anything more.

The End

Next Book in this Series

Book 6: *Bridesmaids and Bodies*
Coming June 2020

OR

Free Prequel: *Vacations and Victims*.
Meet Concetta and Bethany in the
Sapphire Beach prequel.
Available in ebook or PDF format only at:
BookHip.com/MWHDFP

Stay in touch!

Join my Readers' Group for periodic updates,
exclusive content, and to be notified of new releases.
Enter your email address at:
BookHip.com/MWHDFP

OR

Email:
angela@angelakryan.com

Facebook:
facebook.com/AngelaKRyanAuthor

Post Office:
Angela K. Ryan, John Paul Publishing, P.O. Box
283, Tewksbury, MA 01876

ABOUT THE AUTHOR

Angela K. Ryan, author of the *Sapphire Beach Cozy Mystery Series*, writes clean, feel-good stories that uplift and inspire, with mysteries that will keep you guessing.

When she is not writing, Angela enjoys the outdoors, especially kayaking, stand-up paddleboarding, snowshoeing, and skiing. She lives near Boston and loves the change of seasons in New England, but, like her main character, she looks forward to brief escapes to the white, sandy beaches of southwest Florida, where her mother resides.

Angela dreams of one day owning a Cavalier King Charles Spaniel like Ginger, but isn't home enough to take care of one. So, for now, she lives vicariously through her main character, Connie.

Made in the USA
Middletown, DE
13 June 2020